Communion

Jean Blasiar
and
Jonathan Marcantoni

Savant Books and Publications
Honolulu, HI, USA
2011

Published in the USA by Savant Books and Publications
2630 Kapiolani Blvd #1601
Honolulu, HI 96826
http://www.savantbooksandpublications.com

Printed in the USA

Edited by Zachary M. Oliver
Cover by Christie Ussher

13-digit ISBN: 978-0-9832861-4-1
10-digit ISBN: 0983286140

Dedication

Jean Blasiar
"Communion" is a tribute to families: John's, Zach's, mine, everyone's.

Jonathan Marcantoni
For Ali and Tessa, my beloved daughters, and for my amazing and unforgettable wife, Suset, who I carry in my heart everywhere I go.

Acknowledgements

Jean Blasiar

I would like to thank my co-writer, Jonathan Marcantoni, who developed this story with a father's instinct and love, Zachary Oliver—more than an editor, a caring contributor—and Daniel Janik who afforded the three of us this wonderful experience of working together.

Jonathan Marcantoni

I would like to thank Zachary Oliver for his hard work and dedication to this novel. I first worked with Zach as the editor on his book *Falling but Fulfilled* and am thrilled that he returned the favor with such great skill. He is as great an editor as he is a writer, and is also a stand up guy. I wouldn't trust anyone else with my work. Thanks also to Daniel Janik for supporting the novel and its unconventional birth and completion. I also would like to thank my co-author, Jean, for inviting me to join her in telling this story. I have never been big on collaborations, but working with Jean fit like a glove, and I'm honored to have worked with her.

I also wish to thank my wife, Suset, who supports me and keeps me focused; who feeds me both physically and spiritually; and who keeps me grounded while my creative mind wanders. She is my Melanie, a woman I trust completely to keep my home in order, and who I know would never stop searching for me if I were lost.

Prologue

The morning that Melanie and Edward Commons brought their newborn daughter home to Edward's parent's house was an ordinary day during the end of May, 1937. The late spring day in northern Ohio hinted at a summer that was just a few weeks away. Warm enough to shed the heavy winter coats and walk around outside in shirt sleeves, the locals stepped a little lighter and smiled a little easier. The land burst with life, with deep blue sky, green streaks in the grass and trees, and with delicate wildflowers. The fragrant lilac trees burst with blossoms. The air permeated with a vitality that hints at the new life possible for an old house and an elderly couple.

The grandparents, Abigail and Frederick Commons, were standing on the front porch awaiting the arrival of their first grandchild when Edward drove up in his father's old Ford. The baby's mother held the child, draped in a pretty pink hand-knit wrapper, as her husband opened the door with one hand and tenderly took her arm with the other.

"Abbey, Fred, this is your granddaughter, Gemini," the baby's mother proudly announced.

At the sound of the name the grandmother stiffened. Her posture straightened; her head erect. Her righteousness would not allow her to reach out and take that small pink bundle of soft, sweet smelling baby in her arms. "So, you're insisting on that pagan name?" was all that the elderly woman had to say.

In an unexpected move, Fred Commons, the baby's grandfather, reached for the baby and said, "Let me have her."

The baby's father moved quickly to open the screen door for the old man and the baby.

"She's beautiful, Abbey," the baby's mother remarked, trying to draw out her offended mother-in-law.

"Shame she doesn't have a beautiful Christian name. Never was, never will be a Saint Gemini."

The baby's mother, Melanie, prepared for this inevitable confrontation, responded with a question. "What would you like her second name to be?" The young parents had already decided that, to make peace in the family, they would allow Abigail to choose the child's middle name. Melanie shuddered now, regretting this decision.

The name came quickly from her mother-in-law's mouth. "Marie," she said resolutely, her tone dismissing any further discussion on the subject. "After my mother: a saint."

Melanie nodded, not unhappy with the choice. "And we will call her Gem," she said with comparable resolve as she entered the house.

And so, on May 25th, 1937, Gem Marie Commons entered the house of her Grandmother and Grandfather, a home which one day would become a purgatory for the child.

Communion

Chapter One

The old frame house with its wrap around porch had seen considerable upheaval before Gem Marie Commons was carried over the threshold. Immediately, the inside cat became an outside cat. The two upstairs bedrooms were converted into a nursery for Gem and an adjacent bedroom for Edward and Melanie. Abigail and Fred Commons took over the downstairs back sitting room as their own.

"Getting too old to climb those stairs anyway," Fred commented as he and "the Missus," as Fred would always call her, made do with less in the way of room but more in the mouths they would have to help feed.

The upstairs bedroom, directly over the room her

in-laws now occupied, made Melanie most uncomfortable. While the upstairs master bedroom did have a door which offered some privacy, the bed was situated right over her sleeping in-law's heads. Love making in the upstairs bedroom was now, of necessity, restricted in exuberance.

"Some day," Edward would say, "we'll have a home of our own and more children."

"The only way we are going to have more children, darling," Melanie would say, "is if we have a bedroom on the ground floor. Perhaps we could buy a bed spring that doesn't squeak."

"We'll start saving now."

Yet, Melanie knew that it would be many months before money could be spent on non-essentials. Besides, who would tell Abigail that her bed squeaked? It had been good enough for her and Fred, probably also for Abigail's parents before her. "Poor Fred," Melanie often said quietly about her long suffering but always pleasant father-in-law. Everyone in town knew that it took someone with a kind disposition like Fred's to suffer "The Missus's" strong hand all these many years.

"Anyway, we can't afford more children right now." And, of course, Edward was right. So they doted upon the child that they had.

Edward Commons worked as an assistant baker in the Montgomery Bakery in town. Melanie worked part time as an art instructor in the local high school and part time at home as a free lance artist. Fred converted the back sun porch facing east—the morning sun shining gloriously in through the bank of windows—where Melanie could paint from daybreak until it was time to get ready for school. After Gem was put to bed in the evening, Melanie worked by candlelight out in the porch with no electricity, no heat and no one looking over her shoulder. Painting in a heavy old coat of Edward's on the drafty porch, the young wife was happy even though her husband retired at eight o'clock each evening, immediately after carrying Gem on his shoulders to her upstairs room. The baker, still in his twenties, was in the routine of five hours sleep before he opened his eyes, tiptoed out of the house, and walked the half mile into town to work. At seven a.m. each morning, excluding Sundays, the townsfolk of Erieville, Ohio on beautiful Lake Kashuma would awaken to the aroma of freshly baked cinnamon rolls and hot cross buns.

Melanie was a good artist, a very good artist. She portrayed citizens in everyday life with a whimsical flare. Many compared her drawings with those of the famous Norman Rockwell, though Mister Rockwell rode atop the high tide of fame while Melanie was unsuccessfully trying to break into the out-of-reach world of published art. The young woman might have found a niche if such a huge talent as Rockwell's hadn't already beaten her to the head of the line. In 1930s and for the next two decades, there was only one Rockwell and no editor would even consider a second or third rate imitation.

Weekdays were spent working—Melanie at school, Edward at the bakery—but Sunday mornings were reserved for Gem. It was the only morning that Edward could sleep in, but it was also the only time that he and his daughter had together. He looked forward to waking her, helping her dress, bundling her up in winter to wade out into the deep snow, and driving with her to the bakery with the car sliding on the icy streets and Gem laughing. In the chilly bakery—until the ovens warmed the room—the two of them would bake the little buns that Gem loved so much. Her creations had raisins on top of the frosting or cherries, which she added herself, some to the buns, but mostly frosting and cherry juice to her apron, her fingers, nose, and hair.

Sunday mornings were a glorious time together for father and daughter. No one, absolutely no one, was invited to join them, not Melanie, Grand Abbey, or Grandpa Fred.

Just the two of them. They would bring home the buns that Gem didn't eat for the family's Sunday breakfast. It was a very special ritual and one which, during the first three years of Gem's young life, her father never missed, except when the little girl had a fever and her grandmother insisted that she not be taken out of the house.

It was during this period of Gem's young life—her mother and father both away from the house most of the time—that Gem was raised primarily by her "Grand Abbey". Each weekday morning and Saturdays when it wasn't raining, even in the snow, the child would pack up her teddy bears and take them to the makeshift house in the back garden that featured an oil cloth thrown over an old card table Grandpa Fred had given her. It made a fine house for her menagerie of bears. Gem propped up one of the wobbly legs of the card table with a brick from behind the garden and with planted hands on hips declared the enclosure "the teddy bear house".

With her long blonde hair, it was not beyond the realm of possibility that Gem had likened herself to Goldilocks and the playhouse to the home of the three bears.

Gem tidied her teddy bear house each morning while Grand Abbey did the same inside. Grand Abbey delighted in watching her grandchild each morning in her hand-me-down apron busying herself with picking wildflowers, sweeping the leaves and acorns from the playhouse with the little old broom that Grandpa had cut down for her, and setting the mini table—a handmade birthday gift from Grandpa—in the bear's house. She did all this in preparation to ceremoniously serve tea to her inanimate friends.

In winter, it took a great deal longer to bundle the child in leggings and boots, gloves on a ribbon around her neck, through the sleeves of her coat, knitted hat with ear flaps and mittens, and an apron over her coat. And without fail, of course, within the first half hour, the child would be back knocking at the door with her mittened hand to go to the bathroom.

Frederick spent his days in the garage working on some new project, wee chairs for the child and her bears, or the gift he slaved over secretly for the following Christmas, a china closet for her little tin dishes, cups and "silverware". When the back yard thawed sufficiently to turn the ground, Fred marked off a small plot for a vegetable garden for his granddaughter. The earth was still mostly rock, but with some new soil which he was given by a neighbor, and watering, which the little girl insisted she would do, Fred thought the earth might produce a few carrots or radishes for the child to see how things grow, like herself with nourishment, rest, and care. There was no doubt about the little girl giving lots of care and love to her plants as she did to everyone, including her bears.

Grand Abbey argued that Fred was raising the hopes of the child too high. "Nothing," she said, "has ever grown in that garden but weeds. Don't disappoint the child by promising her carrots, you fool."

But the little girl faithfully weeded, once she understood the difference between a weed and a young plant, watered every other day as Fred advised her, and talked to her plants. Both grandparents heard her in the garden telling her plants how important it was to have lots of sunshine, water, and rest if they were going to grow big and strong like her father. Always, she said, "like" or "for" her father. No matter what Grandpa or Grand Abbey did for her, it was always going to be a surprise for her father. And when her father walked in the front door around four every afternoon, after working almost a twelve hour day, the child was at his feet, dragging him outside to see the tops of her plants and then pulling him upstairs by his shirt sleeves to her room to watch the squirrel on the windowsill arrive when the little girl appeared in the window. The squirrel would chatter away and Gem would chatter along with him, first the squirrel, then the little girl, then the squirrel, like a real conversation. Edward Commons had no doubt that it was, in fact, a very real conversation, because, at times, the child would cock her head sideways as though she didn't understand, then the squirrel would chatter away again and the child would laugh and nod her head like she got it, whatever "it" was.

She never told anyone. What transpired between her and the squirrel, the cat who visited the sill at night, the birds who chirped when she walked out into her garden alone, and the frog who croaked when she called to him was between the child and each of them and only them. They made her laugh and, once, made her cry. On that occasion, her father had asked, "Why the tears, little one?" and she had said, "A baby bird has fallen from a nest."

"Show me where," her father had said.

"Not here, daddy," she explained. "Far away."

Edward Commons knew better than to question his daughter about how she knew this. He accepted that the child either had a very active imagination, which would one day be a very good thing for a storyteller, or she was blessed (or cursed) with the ability to communicate with the animal kingdom. "A gift," Edward had called it.

"Rubbish," his mother had said. "She makes things up."

"That… is also a gift," Edward had cautioned and ended that conversation between them.

When the first carrot peeked out of the ground, Gem was delirious. She was still in her nightgown and barefoot, having snuck downstairs after she heard her mother leave the house, her father long gone to the bakery. And there it was, its perfect orange head sticking out of the ground. And another one. Three in all.

"Free," she told her grandpa as she pulled him out of bed and into the garden to see.

Grand Abbey was in the kitchen preparing breakfast that morning. "You'll step on a rock, Gem Marie," she called to the bizarre couple, a sixty year old man and a little girl in nightclothes, both of them barefoot in the back yard. Even when Gem proudly showed her grandmother the three carrots, which her grandfather told her she could pick, Abigail looked away mockingly. "Scrawny," she said.

But Fred washed one of the carrots and gave it to the child to eat. At first, the little girl couldn't bear biting into it, but egged on by her grandfather, she took a small bite.

"Licious!" she declared.

A few days later, red radishes popped up, then the beginnings of lettuce. It was a great celebration that first night that the family sat down at the dinner table and tasted Gem's "salwad". "'Licious," everyone agreed, even Abigail. The child was eating. And that's all her Grand Abbey cared about.

One afternoon when Gem was taking her nap, Fred caught the Missus out inspecting the garden. She had insisted that it was too rocky for anything to grow. Fred wondered, snickering privately to himself, if the Missus thought he buried young carrots and radishes and even small heads of lettuce so their little granddaughter would have the pleasure of seeing them grow.

During her inspection, Abigail looked up into the oak tree at the new growth of the tree. Fred had noticed it only recently himself. This was the tree that they had been advised to remove because of some disease or fungus or some such, that it might conceivably fall in a wind storm and damage the house, but Fred hadn't had the heart to remove the only shade that sheltered the little bear house, and so he had delayed removing the tree for as long as possible. And here, now shading the garden, new leaves, new branches reaching skyward, renewed life that ended all talk about removal.

14

Abigail became accustomed to seeing and hearing Gem talking to her bears, serving them and herself pieces of the hot cross bun which her daddy brought home to her each afternoon from the bakery. When they were naughty, the little girl would scold the bears, sometimes make them sit in a corner of the playhouse, but mostly tell them stories from a book which as yet she could not read, kiss them goodnight, and put them down for a nappy. It was a ritual that no longer concerned the grandmother as it had the first time she heard the child talking to the bears as if they were her children.

Abigail and Fred Commons had only one child, a boy, Edward. They were not accustomed to the fantasies of little girls and their "children". However, Abigail soon became mesmerized by the child and would sit for long periods of time listening to Gem repeat the words she had heard her mother and father, Grand Abbey and grandpa use. One morning as Abigail was peeking behind the curtain from the back bedroom window, she saw movement in the bushes behind the playhouse. Gem had seen it also. The little girl walked to the back of the garden, over the rocks separating the flower beds from the field beyond to the fence that separated the properties.

Upstairs, Grand Abbey screamed. She tried

desperately to open the window but moisture had warped the wood and it was jammed shut.

A small deer appeared at the fence and Gem walked up to it. The grandmother's instinct was to run outside, but she knew that she could not get to her grandchild in time. She watched with lessening fear as Gem walked close to the fence and stared at the deer. As far as Abigail could tell, the little girl did not say a word, but continued to look at the deer, and the deer at her. There was no reason for alarm. The deer couldn't get through or over the fence. It was a small deer, about the size of Gem, and it stood there not moving a muscle as the little girl stared back. A good five minutes passed before the deer turned and slowly walked away beyond the sight of Abigail upstairs.

Moments later, Abigail walked through the back garden to the playhouse where Gem was just putting her bears down for their nap on makeshift beds of old blankets and covers from the attic. Abigail expected Gem to be all talk about the deer, but the child—ignoring her grandmother—talked soothingly to her bears, pretended to turn out the light, put her index finger to her mouth to let her grandmother know that she was not to speak, and walked inside for lunch.

Surely now, Abigail thought as she prepared the

peanut butter and jelly sandwich for her granddaughter. But when nothing was said, Abigail couldn't stand it any longer.

"See anything out in the field this morning?" she asked casually, sitting down opposite the child, moving the small tumbler of milk away from the edge of the table.

Gem looked at her blankly. "What?" she asked.

"In the field," Abigail repeated. "See anything out there this morning?"

To her utter frustration, the old woman watched as the child shook her head, ate her sandwich, and drank her milk. When she finished, she carried her dish and cup to the sink, wiped her mouth on the paper napkin, threw it in the waste basket, and marched upstairs for her nap, leaving her grandmother agape, frustrated and terribly, terribly hurt. Who was she waiting to tell and why not the one who was with her all day every day?

At four o'clock that afternoon when Edward Commons came through the front door carrying the little sack of hot cross buns for the family, Abigail was waiting for him.

Gem was coloring on the floor of what was now her mother's art room. Edward came over and kissed his mother on the cheek. "Where's Gem?" he asked.

Abigail was quite used to her son inquiring about his daughter first before anyone or anything else; used to it, but still offended, especially that morning when she was being ignored by her granddaughter as well.

Abigail closed the door to the parlor. "What is it?" her son asked abruptly. "Is anything wrong?"

"No, nothing is wrong," Abigail began, arms folded over her thick waist and apron. "I want to be with you when you talk to her."

"About what?" Edward asked innocently.

And Abigail told Edward what had happened that morning, about the deer, and most worrisome of all, about the child not telling her grandmother about the deer when the woman had clearly seen for herself the child and the deer not three feet apart.

"Has she ever in her young life seen a deer?" Abigail demanded.

"I don't know," Edward said. "In books, I suppose." He had listened seriously and somewhat anxiously to the story, but now he was trying hard not to smile at the vision of his daughter and a deer. "I'll talk to her," he said, aware of what he felt to be his mother's exaggerated concern.

"Not without me," Abigail added.

And so the two of them approached the sun porch

where Gem was busy with her crayons and a piece of drawing paper that her mother had taped to the floor for her.

"Daddy!" The child ran to her father, grabbed him around the middle of his leg, and clung to him. "Did you bring me a sweet?" she asked, big green eyes looking up at him lovingly.

Edward reached into his coat pocket and took out a lemon drop, one from the basket of sweets for the customers in the front of the bakery. On some days, strawberry was the featured flavor, others cherry, but Gem's favorite, by far, was lemon.

"She'll have holes in her teeth even before they're all in," her grandmother admonished, as she did every afternoon while her grandchild eagerly peeled the sweet and popped it into her mouth, a big smile on her face for her daddy, while enthusiastically slurping the sweet juice from the drop.

"So," her father said, taking her hand and walking over to a footstool to sit down, "tell me about your morning."

"I made beckfas for my family," she said, eliding over the word that gave her the most trouble.

"Your bears."

"Yesth." A slight lisp which the doctor said was normal at age three.

"And then what?"

"Then I shwep their house and put them to bed for nappies."

Edward waited. He took his eyes off his daughter for just a glance at his mother standing nearby.

"Can we play now?" the child asked.

She was not going to mention the deer. Edward wondered if it was because her grandmother was in the room and listening. He didn't know why seeing the deer was a secret, but perhaps if they were alone Gem would tell him.

"Why don't you come upstairs and play in your room while I change my clothes," he suggested as they walked past Abigail. One glance told Edward that Abigail expected a full report of whatever the child told him about the deer and sooner than later.

It was time to start supper by the time Edward and his daughter reappeared in the front parlor. Abigail had already begun peeling potatoes and preparing the chops for the pan. In another half hour Melanie walked through the door and was greeted with a ready table on which an early supper was served. After dinner, Gem was excused to play outside while it was still light. Without a breath, Abigail nodded impatiently at Edward to begin.

Just before Fred stood to excuse himself, Edward made an announcement of quite another sort. "Lots of talk in town about the possibility of war in Europe," he said seriously.

"That has nothing to do with us," Abigail shot back intending it to be the last words on the subject.

"Yes, it has, Mother," Edward countered. "We will be drawn into it."

"You don't know that, sweetheart," Melanie said, putting her hand on her husband's arm. "President Roosevelt..."

"President Roosevelt needs a war," Fred said, piping up uncharacteristically, "to get us out of this depression. Edward is right to be concerned. I would be, too, if I weren't too old to serve."

"Fred, don't talk about things you know nothing about."

"We have to face it," Edward said. "We'll be at war soon."

"Why do you bring it up, Edward?" Melanie said, staring at her usually quiet, easygoing husband who never worried anyone ever.

"I could be called up in a draft," Edward said solemnly. He rose. "It hasn't happened yet, but before it does, mind you, I'll enlist. Two years enlistment is a lot better than four years drafted."

"Bite your tongue!" Abigail shouted. Abigail Commons was not above raising her voice even at the dinner table. "There'll be no more talk about war." And, she quickly redirected the discussion with a quick gulp of air, "Tell us now about the deer."

Melanie and Fred looked at Edward, curious, confused, trying to take in whatever was going on by way of conversation that afternoon.

"What deer?" Melanie said to her husband.

But, before Edward could open his mouth, Abigail broke in with, "There was a deer in the field beyond the house this morning. The child (she always referred to her granddaughter as 'the child') walked up to it."

"Edward!" Melanie gasped, reaching for his hand.

"It was nothing," Edward said.

"The child walked right up to it, no farther than three feet from its head."

"Separated by a fence," Edward was quick to add.

Melanie's head was on a swivel from her mother-in-law to her husband, a frightened look on her face, which

Edward had not assuaged in the least with his non-chalant remark about the fence.

"Did she tell you about it without your asking?" Abigail demanded.

That's really what she wanted to know, Edward thought wearily. Did her granddaughter tell her father willingly what she would not tell her grandmother even when questioned?

"I asked her," Edward admitted.

"And what did she say?"

"She said a deer came to the back fence. That's all." Edward did not add that what his daughter had also told him was, "we talked."

Edward had not pursued the subject with his little girl. They had "talked." His mother had said more than once that not one word came out of the child's mouth, not while she was standing there looking at the deer, not when she was asked about it later. There was no "talk." That admission from his daughter, "We talked," was something Edward decided to keep to himself and think about later, perhaps even bring up again with Gem. And perhaps not.

After Edward's talk about a possible war and draft, the family was too preoccupied with the frightening near future to think about trivial yet curious incidents with "the child".

It did not, however, stop Abigail from thinking back later that evening about some other curious happenings in the past. The cat that had become an outdoor cat the day the baby was carried into the house now kept vigilance on the roof over the front portico from where he could sit and look into the nursery. He could not be lured away from the roof when Gem was in the room, not when she was a baby asleep in her crib, and certainly not during the hours she spent playing with her toys.

The cat would sit on the windowsill for hours and watch. Abigail had even caught the child close up to the window with the cat on the sill on the other side, separated only by the pane of glass. Both of them, the child and the cat, watching each other.

Of course, there were old wives tales about cats and babies, cats staring at babies, cats jumping into cribs smothering babies, killing babies, but Abigail never held any credence to any of them. The cat would never be allowed inside the house again, and that was the end of that. The strange thing about it was the way it seemed content even "obsessed" to sit on the windowsill whenever the child was in the room and watch.

And there were other unexplained incidents,

nothing she attached any significance to at the time, but now added on top of the unexplained event that morning, something to make a note of for the next time. By the light of the moon streaming through the window, Abigail slipped out of bed, careful not to awaken Fred, sat at her desk and wrote in her journal several paragraphs of strange behavior on the part of the child, including those of the cat and the deer.

Abigail wasn't the only one awake in the Commons house that evening. Edward and Melanie made love and then held onto each other. Nothing more was said about enlisting. Everything there was to say about their fear was said by their furious but quiet love making, clinging to each other later as they both slept.

One week later, on a chilly Sunday afternoon in early December while everyone was glued to the radio listening to the news from Pearl Harbor, President Roosevelt declared war on the Japanese.

Edward Commons enlisted in the Army the next day.

Communion

Chapter Two

No argument Melanie or Abigail could ever voice would have convinced Edward not to enlist. To him, the decision was black and white, two years versus four years for the draft, only added to his strong belief that making cinnamon rolls and hot cross buns was not the way to serve one's country.

Edward went so far as to lie on his application about his employment. He was determined *not* to spend his two years in the army in a kitchen. If he was going to join the Armed Forces, he was going to fight. No arguments to the contrary from his wife or his mother would change his mind.

Basic training began on a Monday in January. For his departure, he insisted that Melanie and his mother stay home with Gem, who was still asleep, and keep their lives as close to normal as possible. Only Fred joined his son at the railroad station outside Erieville that cold morning when their lives would change forever. The only thing Fred said to his son was, "Be sure to write to your mother, son."

The old man was desperately trying to hold back tears that morning. Fred Commons wasn't big or strong enough to forcibly detain his son. In his desperate imaginings, the broken man wanted to drag his son home, tie him up and guard him with an armed shotgun should anyone be fool enough to come after him for the draft.

At the end of 1941 and throughout the beginning of 1942, life was not normal anywhere in the United States. Everything was suddenly bustling. Defense plants sprang up everywhere, including a factory just outside Erieville, Ohio. In September, Melanie Commons put on a jump suit and a bandana over her dark, curly hair—a look straight out of a Saturday Evening Post cover by Norman Rockwell—and went to work as a checker in the still-under-construction airplane factory in town. Even Fred Commons had inquired about factory work, but was told he was too old. He seemed to go downhill after that, aging ten years in the two that his son was expected to be overseas and during which his daughter-in-law was helping to build planes to bring their boy home.

In her father's absence, Gem became the baker in the family, working beside her Grand Abbey in the kitchen, rolling out dough, cutting out circles and decorating buns with raisins and frosting. She became quite good at baking, so good that Grandpa built the child a "Hot Cross for the Red Cross" stand in front of their house where the little girl, with her grandpa by her side, would sell her home made hot cross buns for a nickel. The money was sent each week to the Red Cross with a note that Gem Commons, age 5, was selling buns to bring her daddy home.

Gem made a crayon drawing of her and Grandpa selling buns for her daddy. Fred walked proudly with the child to the post office to see that the drawing was posted. Then, they went home to her baking, and to wait for a reply.

About six weeks after Gem sent the drawing to her daddy, Gem and her Grand Abbey were in the kitchen baking. Without any warning, the child suddenly looked up, not *at* her grandmother, but—as Abigail would tell it many times later—*through* her.

"What is it, child?" Abigail asked. "You got a sick

stomach?" Abigail reached for a basin in case the child was about to be sick.

The little girl never said a word. Whatever it was that passed through her mind (or her brain, her grandmother thought), to everyone's horror, the child did not speak again for the rest of the day. Strangely, the spell didn't pass; Gem remained quiet day after day, without a word ever escaping her lips.

Melanie took off work many days to take her daughter to doctors, but no one could find whatever it was that affected the child. She ate, played, slept, bathed, went to school, but wouldn't utter a word.

Gem's teachers were sympathetic, giving the child written assignments when others in her class were called upon to recite. The little girl did not seem to mind the extra work. She ignored the remarks of her classmates who called her a faker. She could not under any circumstances be enticed to speak even though there seemed to be nothing wrong with her. Melanie asked the doctors if it could be related to her daughter's lisp. Was she perhaps self conscious? Had she been teased and refused to embarrass herself again? Fred cashed in an old insurance policy and, with the money he generously handed over, Melanie took Gem to a psychiatrist that the doctors in town recommended.

For three weeks, Melanie attended the sessions with her daughter. She watched every move her daughter made as Gem sat on a sofa and listened to the gentle man who talked to her, but never said a word. Not a smile, a frown, or even a nod that she understood anything that the kind man was saying. There was talk about a psychiatric hospital, but neither Melanie nor Abigail would hear of it. "She'll be okay," her grandmother would say, "when her daddy gets home." But, as the weeks stretched into months, then another year, Abigail began to doubt her own words.

The routine at the house never changed. Gem went about taking care of her family of bears, her dolls, her baking, her homework silently with never another word. She would open the picture books in the playhouse with her bears beside her and noiselessly turn the pages. Silent stories for a silent audience from a silent reader. Those first weeks, Abigail thought focusing on herself, she would lose her mind from all the silence. She made Fred come in the house and do his sanding and shellacking of the bird's nest and the new mailbox where he could look up and talk to her occasionally. Abigail kept up a conversation with the child even though there was never a response. While they were baking, Abbey would ask a question now and then, thinking she might be able to force a response, but the child had either lost her speech or just stubbornly refused to use it. There was nothing any of those doctors found that convinced Abigail that the child had experienced some sort of seizure.

"She's perfectly normal," the frustrated Grand Abbey would tell anyone in earshot. "She's just... quiet."

But, quiet didn't begin to describe the little Gem.

Something also happened between "the child" and her grandmother. It began with the deer that the child wouldn't talk about with her. Then, little things about not sharing her enthusiasm for her garden with her Grand Abbey as she did with her grandpa, began to eat at Abigail. The child and grandmother grew apart. "You don't understand little girls," Fred would say.

And the missus would return, "And I suppose you do."

Indeed, of the two of them, Fred did.

Chapter Three

The letter arrived by a uniformed courier who pulled up to the house on a Saturday morning, June 23rd, 1943. Melanie knew before the door opened that the man in uniform was bringing the dreaded letter.

Abigail opened the door and stoically accepted it. She said nothing to the uniformed man. Fred came up behind Abigail. It was as though they were expecting it.

Missing.

Not dead. *Missing.*

It was, in Abigail and Fred's way of thinking, not the bad news. There had been no letters from Edward for a month. The courier could have brought the bad news, the bad news which no one would ever allow to be said aloud.

As long as that news wasn't put into the air between them, whether by government correspondence or by their own loss of faith, they could look at it this way: there'd be no little flag with a star in the center of their window announcing to the world that their son was killed in action.

The neighbors had seen the car pull up. They rushed over to Abigail and Fred and Melanie as soon as the car drove away.

Missing.

The word etched in Melanie's brain. If Gem understood what was happening, she didn't cry. She didn't speak, and she didn't cry, but she didn't let anyone but grandpa hold her for a very long time.

Missing.

At the factory, Melanie threw herself into getting ahead, trying to save enough money to take Gem to Boston or New York where there were famous doctors, expensive doctors, who might be able to help her daughter. The young mother started out as a checker, someone who checked the time cards of the factory workers on the assembly line, computed their hourly rate plus overtime, and delivered the figures to payroll. Six months later, Melanie had advanced to a desk job in the payroll department. Not long after that promotion, she became Head of the Payroll Department. Her quick promotion was no fluke, no necessary elevation due to a lack of worthwhile workers with a flair for supervisory work. Applicants were coming from miles away, moving into trailers and temporary housing, just for the good jobs. And this job, Head of the Payroll Department, was a very important job.

Quite by accident, Melanie's fellow workers became aware of her artistic talent. One year after Melanie started working at the factory, at lunch where all the employees came together, the workers were encouraging everyone to enter the contest to see who could come up with a caricature for the first fully assembled military plane to come off the line.

As a lark, Melanie entered the contest with a larger than life caricature of the famous photograph of Betty Grable, sassily posing with her gorgeous legs in a white bathing suit, hands on hips looking over her shoulder.

The painting caught the attention of Carl Hesseman, a top executive at the factory.

"Good morning."

The tall, blond man with the cool-as-ice blue eyes was standing in front of Melanie's desk one morning addressing her. Melanie had no idea who he was.

"May I help you?" she asked. The only people who ever visited Melanie in her cubicle at the back of the office were the clerks or, occasionally, a worker with a complaint about his paycheck.

"Are you Melanie Commons?"

"Yes, I am." *What had she done?*

"I'm Carl Hesseman, General Manager of Simmons Aircaft."

Oh, my God! She didn't know what to do, stand up, put out her hand, or crawl under the desk like she wanted to do. It was him, the one she heard about.

"Have I…? Is there…?"

Carl Hesseman laughed. "I'm here to pay you a compliment."

Melanie didn't understand. "Me… sir?"

"If you are the Melanie Commons who submitted the drawing for our fighter airplane. Yes, you. Very nice work. I wanted to tell you in person."

"Oh." Melanie's heart was beating so fast she didn't trust her voice.

"You won the contest."

Her eyes opened wide (she felt them), her mouth opened (she knew it), her jaw dropped (she felt it). She was aware that she was standing there with her mouth open.

How unattractive.

"Congratulations." He held out his hand to her.

Somehow Melanie's brain engaged enough to lift her hand. His hand was soft, very well manicured. Looking down at their hands, she grabbed a much needed breath. By the time he said, "You won the contest!" Melanie had stopped breathing.

"It was…" she started to say.

"Very professional," he continued. "You're an artist."

Melanie hesitated to admit to that. "I paint…" she said, "at home."

"I would love to see your art some day. But, for now, I want your permission, your written permission, to license this painting."

"License?"

"Yes. I assume you are aware, Miss Commons… Is it *Miss* Commons?"

"No. It's Mrs."

Did he flinch? Melanie was sure she saw something in his eyes, a narrowing, a… *was that disappointment.* "My husband's in the army," she said. "Overseas."

"Wonderful. I mean, what a wonderful thing he is doing for his country, but hard on his wife."

"And little girl," Melanie added. "We have a child, Gem"

"Gem?"

"Short for Gemini, the month of her birth."

"Ah." He didn't appear to be taken back by what Abigail called the *pagan name*. "You do know that the winner of the contest will have his or her art reproduced on the first P40 fighter plane to come off our assembly line. And this, my dear, is the winning entry." He held up what Melanie hadn't realized was in his left hand, her drawing of Betty Grable.

There was no one in the office to see the Head of the Payroll Department go pale, totter, and nearly collapse if the tall blond man in the expensive three piece suit hadn't reached out to catch her.

Mr. Hesseman laughed as he lowered Melanie into her chair. "Such an attractive response, joy. I assume it is joy that has overcome you."

"Oh." She sighed, trying hard to catch her poise. "Joy. And shock."

"Perhaps a cup of coffee?"

"No, thank you. I just need a minute to catch my breath. It was a whim. The workers on the line suggested that I enter the contest."

"I'll thank them in my remarks to the crowd at the unveiling."

"The unveiling?"

"I assume the Assistant Head of Payroll can take over the department while you, our winner, are busy reproducing this" he held up the drawing, "in living color six feet tall."

"Six…"

"I'm sure you can do it. If you're feeling up to it now, I'll show you your shark-like canvas. Don't let the teeth scare you."

Melanie remembered saying, "Teeth?" as she walked with Mr. Hesseman that morning out through the Payroll Department to the applause of her fellow workers who obviously had been listening at the open door, and followed him down through the offices where word had spread and applause followed and into the factory where all of the men and women on the assembly line were standing and applauding their entrance. If it hadn't been for Mr. Hesseman's strong hold on her arm, Melanie knew that she would have succumbed to the floating feeling she had that this was all some lovely, unexpected dream from which she hoped never to awake.

For the next two weeks, Melanie arrived on the

floor of the assembly plant every morning with her paint, brushes, and turpentine. A ladder awaited her and a scaffolding which had been erected with steps that allowed her to draw and then paint the likeness of Betty Grable from the top down. When she was ready to expose more of Miss Grable, two workers who became her very good friends—Tony and Marty—would help her down, lower the scaffolding and reposition the shelf on which she stood.

There was a great deal of whistling and some risqué remarks spoken behind hands to their mouths as first the upper shape of Miss Grable and then the lower began to emerge. There was even singing, "Oh, You Beautiful Doll..." and "Pretty Baby". Melanie thought for sure that during all this ruckus Mr. Hesseman would come out on the upper balcony overlooking the factory floor, where she frequently saw him stand, and announce over the loudspeaker, "Get back to work!" But, he didn't.

"It's all part of the spirit," one of her new friends, Tony, told her while adjusting the scaffolding. "They want us to get into it. For him." He pointed to a man taking pictures and making notes on the sideline. Melanie had seen him before, observing the painting, but she didn't know who he was. "That's Jimmy Winchell," her other friend on the scaffold, Marty, said. "He's covering the unveiling for the wire services." He leaned in to whisper, "We hear this is going to make big waves in Washington." At which, Melanie nearly dropped her brush.

"Careful," Marty said. "That's very important work you're doing on behalf of the war. This baby's going to drop bombs on the Führer."

Melanie glanced up at the balcony. Carl Hesseman was standing there, smoking. When their eyes met, Melanie managed a weak smile and a slight wave. Mr. Hesseman smiled back at her. Two weeks later, when the final touches were put on Miss Grable's very high heels and Melanie was satisfied that the scaffolding could come down, she stood there looking critically at the painting. The entire floor erupted in applause and whistles with one particular admirer applauding from the balcony. Melanie looked up and took notice, then turned and shook hands with those around her.

Abigail, Fred, and Gem were invited to the unveiling. They were seated in the grandstand outside the closed hangar along with the press and families of the assembly workers. The dedication was to be followed by a reception honoring Melanie.

For the special occasion, Melanie chose her best dress and high heels, which she hadn't worn since the evening before Edward left to join the Army. Her long brown hair was done up in a snood. Her lips painted. Her nails manicured (after hours of soaking in paint remover). Her legs, glamorous in silk stockings (a gift from Tony and Marty), reminded her what it felt like to be a woman. Her heart beat excitedly as Mr. Hesseman helped her up into the decorated topless jeep to follow the plane onto the tarmac.

A band was playing, the noise of the crowd was so loud as the huge hangar doors opened that Melanie almost missed what Mr. Hesseman was saying.

"I'm sorry," she said, holding onto her Sunday best hat.

"I said, you look especially beautiful today."

She looked at him, into his eyes, his thigh touching hers in the small front seat of the jeep. She smiled and turned quickly to the roaring crowd and flashing bulbs, but not before she had taken too long a time looking into Mr. Hesseman's eyes. Tony and Marty, who had seen the look exchanged between the honoree and the boss, looked at each other, elbowed, and winked. Fortunately, Abigail, in the stands, did not see the exchange, either Melanie's and Mr. Hesseman's or Tony and Marty's.

At the reception in Melanie's honor in the hangar after the parade, Mr. Hesseman was introduced to Abigail,

Fred, and to Gem, who was holding a small American flag. It was difficult for Gem to appreciate what was going on, but Fred took her and a glass of champagne over to the plane and explained that the painting had been done by her mother. It all seemed too much excitement for the little girl, who clung to her grandpa, lifting her arms up for him to hold her, shielding her eyes from everyone and especially the big plane with the shark-like face and scary teeth. Fred chalked up the child's unusually unfriendly manner to the crowd and to her mother being mobbed by well-wishers, but Abigail saw the look in her granddaughter's eyes when Mr. Hesseman tried to take her granddaughter away from Fred for a picture.

"Children sense," Abigail said to Fred. She watched Carl Hesseman the rest of the afternoon like a hawk, especially when he was taking Melanie by the arm—once with his arm around her waist—and introducing her to dignitaries in the crowd.

It was Mr. Hesseman who suggested that afternoon that Melanie lose her hat, don a pair of overalls, keep her high heels and her snood, face the camera with fists on her hips, feet spread apart, in what would become one of the most famous poses of the war. The iconic photographs perfectly expressed the effort of women on the job working to end the war, to support their fathers, brothers, and husbands fighting for freedom so far from home.

After that afternoon, Melanie Commons made a one eighty detour on her spiraling way up the promotion ladder at the Simmons Airplane Factory. Her career in the payroll department was over; fate had made other plans. On magazine covers and in the newspapers, Melanie's "nose art", as it would be called, was splashed across America. She was commissioned by the management of the factory for six more paintings—the Flying Tigers, Jolly Rogers, Moby Dick, Pluto, Mickey Mouse and Betty Boop. Never forgetting that the demand for this kind of specialized art would come to an end with the end of the war, Melanie nevertheless rode the tide of success for two exciting years. Mr. Hesseman made sure that Melanie received full credit for the nose art craze. He even suggested that Melanie put together a collection of her artwork for a book which he would help her get published. It took all of Melanie's time at work and at home to keep up with the demand, time that before this craze, had been spent with her daughter. Melanie would often tell Gem that she knew the child understood how important it was to their future that mommy make as much money as possible now.

Being successful was exciting and new to Melanie.

She loved the attention and certainly enjoyed the increase in pay. When she wasn't working in the art room at the factory, she was working in the sun room at home on sketches for the next planes coming off the line.

Not everyone at home was ecstatic for Melanie. Her daughter didn't understand Mommy's "work" and her mother-in-law, although she appreciated the extra money coming in now with Fred out of work, resented the attention her daughter-in-law was getting while her husband was thousands of miles away.

Missing.

It was during this period when Melanie was gone so many hours, day and night working on her art collection, that Abigail was alone with the child. One couldn't help but notice things, she told herself. She wasn't spying, but she was alone most days while Fred was off piddling with his woodwork in the garage, and who did she have to look out for if not the child.

The child's preoccupation with nature and animals became increasingly worrisome to her grandmother. Fred had tilled a larger garden for Gem to grow a few more vegetables. At first, Abigail was grateful. It gave Fred something to do, turn the soil, sift out the stones, add fertilizer, and teach his adoring granddaughter how to plant, weed, and care for her "crop". Gem tended her garden every morning before school and every afternoon. Fred erected a scarecrow to keep away the big birds who sat in the trees surrounding the yard, watching, and waiting for the first sign of food. Abigail even donated one of her old dresses off the wash line for the scarecrow. In the print dress with a clothesline for a belt and one of Abigail's old Sunday hats on top of the head, the straw trussed figure had more than a slight resemblance to the grand dame of the house. Fred never said a word, but it made him smile when Abbey wasn't around.

Missing.

Months passed with no word.

Three years almost to the day that Edward left the house that terrible January morning, Melanie asked Abigail if she minded if Mr. Hesseman came to dinner on Sunday.

The frightened young wife approached the subject after dinner one evening when Gem was outside watering her plants, but before Fred took off for wherever it was he disappeared to until dark.

The look that Abigail gave Melanie could have frozen boiling water on the stove. Fred got up, said he had work to do in the garage, and both Abigail and Melanie let him go without a word.

"He wants to show you and Fred the book that is being published with my drawings," Melanie said shakily, trying to soften the outrage that she could see building in Abigail. "It's all perfectly..."

"Respectable?" her mother-in-law added gravely.

The word was out there ripping the silence, echoing in the void that followed it, and seemed to draw a line down the middle of the table, respectable on Abigail's side, a suspiciously non-respectable request from Melanie on the other. Not having the heart or the temerity for taking sides against her mother-in-law ever, Melanie conceded quietly, "Never mind, Abbey. You and Fred can see it when it's published along with everyone else." She got up, picked up her plate, and headed out of the dining room only to be stopped by Abigail's officious voice.

"What do Jewish people eat?"

Melanie froze. Without looking around, she replied, "Mr. Hesseman isn't Jewish and he said he would like to bring dinner."

"I provide dinner for guests in my home," was Abigail's response. And with that, she stood.

Nothing more was said until later that evening when Melanie walked past the parlor where Abigail was reading. "Good night," Melanie said as she always did before retiring.

"Five o'clock Sunday," Abigail said curtly. "We eat early in this house."

Melanie nodded. She half wished she'd never even suggested it, but now she had and he was coming and, "Oh, Lord," she thought, "pray for me."

Chapter Four

Carl Hesseman called at the Commons house promptly at five o'clock on the following Sunday. He brought flowers for Abigail, a bottle of wine for Fred and marking pens in every color imaginable for Gem along with a roll of butcher paper. Abigail thanked Mr. Hesseman dutifully for the flowers. Fred winked, smacked his lips, shook Mr. Hesseman's hand and suggested that they open the fine bottle of wine. It wasn't often that alcohol was served in the Commons house, but that afternoon Abigail did not speak against it.

Fred left the parlor to open the wine. Abigail excused herself to the kitchen to find a vase for her flowers.

At arm's length, Gem took the roll of paper and the pens in thirty two different shades and headed for the sun porch.

"You couldn't have brought Gem anything she loves more than drawing materials," Melanie said to Mister Hesseman. She invited him to sit down on the slipcovered sofa and then seated herself in a chair opposite him.

Melanie commented on the lack of snow so far that winter and Mr. Hesseman agreed. Mr. Hesseman said that he hadn't been in this part of Erieville before but he thought it was a very nice neighborhood to raise a child, and Melanie agreed. Abigail soon joined them. She put a tray of small glasses on the table between the sofa and the chairs and the three of them waited silently for Fred to bring in the wine.

Fred stuck his head into the room and asked Abigail if she would come into the kitchen for a minute. Sensing what might be the problem, Mr. Hesseman asked if he could help uncork the wine. Fred jumped at his offer.

When the two men returned a few minutes later, the wine was uncorked and Mr. Hesseman did the honor of pouring. When they each had a small quantity in the small glasses, Mr. Hesseman raised his glass in a toast. "To Melanie's successful launch as a published artist." Of course, everyone drank to that.

Abigail set her glass down after a tiny sip. "And where is this book we've been hearing about?" she asked.

"In the car," Mr. Hesseman said. "Shall I bring it in now?"

"I believe it can wait," Abigail said soberly. "The roast can't. I'd like everyone to be seated at table."

Mr. Hesseman held Melanie's chair opposite him, then Abigail's chair opposite Fred, then he moved to hold Gem's chair, next to her mother, but the child had managed on her own. During the meal, Gem never once looked directly at Mr. Hesseman seated across the table, but he and everyone else at the table had the uncomfortable feeling that she was.

The executive was, as always, well dressed in a grey suit, pinched collar shirt, vest, striped tie and highly polished shoes. Melanie noticed in the parlor that when Mr. Hesseman sat down, his legs above his socks were not displayed. The young wife had never seen socks that length before, but she would hereafter look upon the white legs of men above their socks as shoddy.

"Are you retired, Mr. Commons?" It was a natural question, no reason not to inquire, but breaking the silence as it did, it seemed pointed, even personal.

"Yes, I am," Fred responded, eyes averted from the

executive.

Melanie piped up with, "Fred worked in Miller's Hardware store in town."

"Forty five years," Fred added, his head over his plate, eyes on his food.

"Handy man to have around," Mr. Hesseman said. "And your husband?" he surprised everyone by asking Melanie. "What was his occupation before he joined the Army?"

"He was a baker," Melanie said. She said it softly, without pride, Abigail thought, without any respect whatsoever for her son's livelihood.

"A very good baker," Abigail felt compelled to add. She glanced at Gem beside her mother and for just an instant she thought she saw movement from her granddaughter that she might be about to speak. Abigail put her fork down and stared at the child, but that movement, the child's little chest expanding with a breath before she might join the conversation passed without a sound. *She's faking,* Abigail thought at that moment. She never expressed that opinion to anyone, though she had thought it many times before. At that moment, she felt certain. *She's faking.*

Melanie mentioned her daughter's baking and the

stand that Fred had built to sell her hot cross buns and the check that was sent every Monday morning to the Red Cross.

From either shyness or embarrassment at being singled out, the little girl in her best Sunday dress with bows in her hair did not look up. If she could feel the eyes of the man across the table staring at her, she gave no indication.

"That's our Gem," Fred piped in. "Our little jewel."

Abigail glared down the table. She never allowed any reference to the child's nickname likened to pagan adornments to be uttered while she was around, but for the moment she let it pass. Fred would no doubt hear about it later when they were alone.

"It's such a pretty name," Mr. Hesseman said. With a look, Abigail dared anyone at the table to agree.

The rest of the meal proceeded with Mr. Hesseman commenting on the excellent meal, the first home made meal he'd had in a very long time.

"Why is that, Mr. Hesseman?" Abigail prodded. "Don't you have family?"

Well, of course, he has family, Melanie wanted to strike back. Everyone has family, but, "No, I don't," came out of Mr. Hesseman's mouth even while Melanie was trying to form a less confrontational way of saying what she wanted to say.

"My parents live in Bonn," he said. "And I'm not married."

"Bonn?" Abigail picked up.

"Germany," Carl Hesseman said.

He could not have said anything more disagreeable if he'd said, "My parents are Jewish," which Melanie had assured her mother-in-law he was not.

Germany, where Edward Commons was stationed, where his last letter was postmarked, so far away from this dinner table and the awkward and idle conversation stumbling around the room.

Missing.

Prisoner of war camps, German-occupied Yugoslavia, Poland, France, the drums from the newsreels, the "Heil, Hitler" goose-stepping Gestapo. The Führer. Everything heinous, despicable, feared and hated by the Commons, was German. A meat market in town owned by a fat, friendly neighbor was forced to close because he was German. Melanie felt a chill down her spine as Abigail stood to clear the table.

The evening was lost. Nothing Mr. Hesseman could say could diffuse the heaviness, the pall that fell on the house like death. Mr. Hesseman went to the car after dinner and brought in the galleys of the book which he and Melanie had submitted and had been accepted by a New York publisher. It should have been a glorious occasion to celebrate, toast, and share. Instead, it was politely received, gratuitiously admired, and abjectly dismissed.

Mr. Hesseman left the house at seven thirty. Abigail's grandmother's dishes were washed, dried and put away again for the next big occasion. No one said a word. It was becoming the house of silence, from the child, from the in-laws, from Germany. After Mr. Hesseman left the Commons' house that evening, Abigail and Melanie got into it with little or no regard for how loudly they spoke, angry words wafted upstairs, and were overheard by Gem who was sitting on the landing, listening.

Melanie started up the stairs in tears after a particularly nasty tirade by Abigail. Gem barely made it into her room, closing the door quietly behind her and jumping into bed before her mother ran into the master bedroom and slammed the door behind her. Another bang came not long thereafter from Abigail slamming the door to the downstairs bedroom as well.

Outside in the workshop off the garage, Fred shook his head and began hand sanding the china closet he was making for Gem. He understood, but wanted no part of the exchange.

His first attempt to win over the Commons's family not coming off as well as it might have, Mr. Hesseman volunteered to try again with fireworks and a special dinner for the Fourth of July. The family would be marching in the town's parade. Gem was ready with her wagon, which Fred had helped her decorate, and her flag. Melanie took lots of pictures, which she planned to study for a Fourth of July painting she hoped to sell to the New Yorker, despite the fact that Norman Rockwell had several quite famous covers already. Still, Melanie had an idea of a particular kind of painting she envisioned and that morning she was busy taking shot after shot of Gem, her wagon, a neighbor's dog and what folks were calling the "little people's parade."

At four o'clock, Mr. Hesseman arrived with a box full of fireworks from snakes to rockets which he proceeded to shoot off with Gem watching. The loud blasts of the rockets frightened the little girl. One rocket landed on the roof of the house and if it hadn't been for Fred's quick action with the garden hose, it might have been a very short evening, which, in retrospect, would have been better than what happened.

As Mr. Hesseman lit still another rocket, Gem

begged her mother silently, running to her with her hands over her ears, to tell him to stop. Finally, Melanie told Mr. Hesseman that the sound was frightening Gem.

Round two of Hesseman's efforts to win over the family was also turning into a dud. But, Hesseman still had his piece de resistance, the roasted pig dinner, which was delivered to the house right on time at five o'clock. The pig was covered with a grand silver dome and unveiled only after it was deposited on the picnic table in the Commons's backyard.

Everyone was waiting for the big surprise. "Ta da!" Mr. Hesseman announced as he removed the dome and the pig with an apple in its mouth was revealed in all its lifeless glory. For the first time in three years, the family heard Gem's voice. She screamed and ran into the house. Abigail swooned. Melanie covered the pig quickly with the dome. Fred, trying to hold onto the Missus, shouted a very bad word indeed.

The party ended on that note. Later, Melanie brought a plate of macaroni and cheese up to Gem, but she refused to eat. Her mother tried to explain what it was on the platter. She insisted that it just "looked like a pig", but the little girl looked at her mother with what could only be construed as distrust in her young eyes.

It was no good. Nothing Melanie said would move the child out of her room. Abigail was too overwrought to even try. Fred, striking out with his attempts to ameliorate the situation, eventually gave up.

But Carl Hesseman did not give up his quest to insinuate himself into the Commons family, particularly with Melanie. Melanie only agreed to meet him for dinner after work and arrived home alone having been dropped off at the end of the block, but Abigail knew when she walked in where she'd been and with whom.

Chapter Five

No longer the ebullient child of age three when she was frequently asked by her family to stop talking long enough to eat, Gem was a mute of four years duration who spoke not a word; an obedient, complacent, sad child who regressed more and more into her world of pets and play. Her mother, with much misgiving and a fair amount of guilt, finally placed her into a special school for children with disabilities.

Melanie ranked as a Designer at the factory with a considerable increase in salary, enough to afford the special school for her daughter. The distraught, anxious young mother was made increasingly aware of her daughter's agony over the absence of her father, a situation that Melanie and her teachers set out to rectify. Evenings were spent with Gem, going over her school work, reading books, and making up stories until the child once again felt close to her mother.

At first, it was startling to Melanie to learn about Gem's animal friends. The child had silent conversations with them. Melanie would sit at her window upstairs and watch Gem in the garden below with her bears, her pet turtle and fish in the pond, and frequently at the back of the garden with something that Melanie could not see. Fred told her that the animal beyond the fence was the doe—a small and perfectly harmless creature—that appeared whenever Gem came outside.

One day, Fred said, he caught a look at the deer when his granddaughter had no idea that her grandpa was anywhere around. Fred told Melanie that he was prepared to frighten away the animal if it looked like Gem was in any danger; but instead, he stayed to watch her and the deer spend long periods of time together, no sounds, no touching, just being together. When the child went back to her bears, Fred said he heard a rustle in the brush and when he looked again, the deer was gone.

At the factory, Melanie managed to keep Mr.

Hesseman at bay, informing him that she was needed at home in the evenings and the weekends to care for her daughter who was going through a particularly stressful period without her father. And, she finally had to tell him, the child felt threatened by the presence of another man attentive to her mother.

Carl Hesseman said, of course, that he understood. When Melanie found him cozying up to the new girl in payroll, it surprised her pleasantly that all she felt was relief.

The PICTORIALS OF WORLD WAR II was released in September. With her little girl at her side, her own pencil in her hand, Melanie signed copies of the book with a distinctive signature and drawing on a Saturday afternoon at the local bookstore. For a period of about two weeks, Melanie was quite the attraction in town, speaking at the Women's Club and the Elk's Hall, under her mother-in-law's disapproving eye, signing copies of the book at work, avoiding Mr. Hesseman's roving eye, and depositing the royalty checks faithfully each month into a special account for Gem's education.

The new girl in Payroll gave notice suddenly. Mr. Hesseman once again tried to hit on Melanie. He had been the one who saw her book through to being published and for that she was very grateful, but his constant appearance at wherever she was in the factory was not only annoying, but embarrassing. Tony and Marty who continued to work with her as she transposed the sketches into the finished product on the planes were powerless to help Melanie as long as they wanted to keep their jobs, which they desperately needed to support their families.

"No, don't do anything to make him think you disapprove," Melanie told them. "I think he could be cruel." It was something in his eyes, those eyes that she felt undress her, devour her, whenever she dared look at him. It was a very lucrative job as Art Designer for the planes and, though she longed to see the end of the terrible war, when it ended Melanie knew that she would be unemployed. What would she do about the special school for Gem then? How would she pay the tuition? There were no other markets, as far as she could tell, for her kind of art.

It was Marty who suggested the comics. "Develop your own character," he said. "Like Popeye."

"Or Lil Abner," Tony suggested. "Let's think of something."

"You're very good at drawing women," Marty commented. "And there aren't any women comic characters. What about a comic strip about who you are?"

Melanie had to laugh. She was putting the finishing touches on Betty Boop when Marty made his comment. "And who am I, Marty?" she asked. "Who do you think I am?"

"Who do I think you are? I think you're a beautiful young artist who went to work in a factory during the war and started painting portraits on planes."

"And you have a love life," Tony threw in, causing Melanie's brush to shake.

"Tony! I'm married!"

"In real life. This is in the comic strip. You have lots of men, all too old because that's all that's left at home, the war having taken all the young men overseas." It was a jab at Hesseman, Melanie knew that. Of course, Hesseman wasn't that old. She wondered more than once how he had avoided the draft.

"Or 4F," Tony said.

Melanie replaced her brushes for the day. Tony on one side and Marty on the other, they helped her dismount from the scaffolding. "I'll think about it," she said, smiling at both of them, hoping they didn't see the blush she felt burning her cheeks.

Having nearly completed the last of her assigned drawings, with no more commissioned, Melanie realized that her contribution to the war effort may, indeed, have come to an end. She wouldn't go back to the Payroll Department where Mr. Hesseman could pop in on her, alone in her office, any time he felt like seeing her. She would be powerless to stop those advances, him being her boss and all. No, if this was going to be her last piece of work, then she would definitely be looking for something else to do.

A comic strip. Work at home. She couldn't stop thinking about it. A beautiful artist who paints on planes. Maybe. She certainly had stories to tell. The artist would have a boy friend (not a husband) overseas. She would be a detective. On more than one occasion, Melanie did pause in her work to watch as the factory workers busily assembled the parts to the various sections of the plane. High up on her scaffold she could see them at their tasks, mindlessly, hour after hour mechanically repeating the same job, putting a screw here, tightening it, testing it, picking up another screw, a wrench. What if they didn't tighten the screw? What if the screw came loose in the assembly of the plane without the quality control people catching it? What if someone... a German perhaps... had infiltrated the factory to sabotage the planes? The movies were full of sabotage stories. Spies were everywhere. "Loose lips sink ships." What if "Loose screws sabotaged planes?"

That evening, Melanie disappeared after dinner to her studio. Gem watched her mother become absorbed in her work once again, an "idea" Melanie told her family at dinner for a new career.

Abigail ushered Gem quietly out of her mother's studio. If a new career took Melanie away from the factory and that horrible German, Abigail was all for it. "Let's go in the kitchen," she said to Gem. "We'll bake something delicious for breakfast. Cinnamon buns."

When after two more weeks no further commissions for paintings came forth from management, Melanie bit the bullet and handed in her resignation. As she knew she would be, she was immediately summoned to Carl Hesseman's office.

"What's this?" he asked. "You're quitting?"

"There doesn't seem to be anything more for me to do."

"Nonsense. I admit that we haven't had a requisition for any more planes. Just between you and me, I believe this war is winding down."

Did he seem disappointed? Don't jump to conclusions. He's probably worried about his job.

"We can only hope," Melanie said gamely.

"Yes. Of course. But... it does put the need for this factory in jeopardy. We might retool and make... refrigerators, God save us. Or televisions, which I hear are the next wave. Something will come up."

"But nothing that will be needing the kind of work for which I'm suited."

"I will always find a job for you, my dear. There's..."

"Actually, Mr. Hesseman-" She always called him Mr. Hesseman even on that occasion when he took her to dinner, just the two of them. "I have submitted some art work and it's been accepted."

"Wonderful! Tell me about it." He got up from his very large chair behind his enormous desk and held a chair for Melanie to sit down, but she remained standing.

"It isn't anything I feel I can talk about yet," she began, "just a lark, but it has potential. I'll have to devote all of my time for now, getting started."

"You don't trust me?"

"Oh- of course, I trust you. I just can't-"

"Remember, I was the one who saw to it that your paintings were included in the book of World War II art, which has been a nice little income for you, hasn't it?"

"Yes, certainly it has. It's allowed me to afford the

special school for my daughter, but this is-"

"Why don't we discuss it over dinner? I'll pick you up in the parking lot at six."

The parking lot, where everyone could see her getting into his car. She recalled the last occasion, when he invited her to dinner, and she met him in the parking lot after work. Several women who worked on the assembly line were walking behind her, saw her get into Mr. Hesseman's car, and giggled. The next morning Melanie swore that everyone on the line was looking up at her on the scaffold and whispering.

"I'm afraid I can't," she said boldly. "I need to get home to my daughter."

Mr. Hesseman sighed deeply, unable to hold it in, not a sigh out of disappointment, a sigh with rancor for Melanie's constant talk about and concern for her impossible daughter. He had faked liking the child on the two occasions he visited their house. In fact, if the truth be known, Carl Hesseman loathed children with their dirty hands. No telling where those hands had been. And their snotty noses. It made his skin crawl to think about them. He had envisioned Melanie's little girl living with her grandparents while her mother and her mother's "sponsor" if you will, traveled. To Germany, perhaps. To the green fields and the castles he'd known as a child, where civilization had evolved into a higher form of gentility and children were kept in their place with nannies and boarding schools, such as he had experienced before he reached adulthood.

"I can help you with your new line of work," Hesseman said. "I have influence in many spheres."

But Melanie shook her head. She had to get out of there. "I'm afraid not," she heard herself saying. She was shaking inside, but determined not to give in.

"You are an ungrateful girl," Carl Hesseman said sourly. Melanie saw the corner of his mouth curl up in a frightening look she'd never seen before, but somehow knew he was capable of projecting. This was the real Carl Hesseman, the German, not Carl Hesseman, the brilliant designer of aircraft. This Carl Hesseman before her now would make a wonderful villain in her comic strip if she ever had the nerve to use it. She knew that she wouldn't. And, indeed, she admonished herself, that would be ungrateful.

In the end, after a tirade about how he had made the ungrateful girl famous, Carl Hesseman told Melanie to, "Clean out your locker and get out!"

The staff in the outside office had obviously heard.

Melanie walked down the corridor of open cubicles, where everyone was suddenly busily typing and deliberately not looking in her direction.

The locker room was empty. Everything about the atmosphere was unfriendly. Melanie put her few personal items, some lunch containers, an extra pair of shoes, a sweater, makeup, a comb and brush and mirror in a sack, closed the locker, and left. Tony and Marty were on the floor, unaware of what had occurred in Hesseman's office. Melanie left without seeing them, but she would send them a note addressed to Personnel explaining. Maybe they would get it and maybe they wouldn't. For a young woman who saw such fame and recognition during her tenure at the factory, she was leaving under a cloud, but it was with a feeling of freedom that Melanie Commons left the factory that morning and headed for the bus.

Communion

Chapter Six

Nobody loved *Warrior Woman* more than little Gem Commons. A super woman in a red, white and blue costume, tight as another skin, buxom, long hair and boots emerged from Melanie's sketch pad one evening while Gem was sitting beside her on the floor of her studio.

"Warrior Woman," Melanie said, holding up the drawing to her daughter. Gem's eyes brightened. When she stopped talking two years earlier, another facet of the child's personality took over, her expressions. She was born with beautiful green eyes that changed from light to dark depending upon her mood and, sometimes, even from light green to light blue, depending upon the color she wore.

More than anything, they reflected her attitude. Until that evening when Melanie showed her the drawing, she had not seen joy in her daughter's expression like that. The child took the sketchpad, studied it, and silently laughed. Her little body shook as she scrunched up her shoulders, her mouth and her eyes in a joyous expression that was both naughty and wonderful. It was almost like she shouldn't like it because the woman wasn't wearing very many clothes, but it was so much fun.

Melanie began talking to her daughter about how *Warrior Woman* saved people in trouble, swooping down and sweeping them up just as they were about to step in front of a car or their car was about to fall over a washed-out bridge. The stories fascinated the little girl who sat on the floor and listened attentively as her mother talked.

It kept the young mother at home and that's all that Abigail Commons cared about. Comics were nonsense. Nothing respectable would come of it, but if it kept the mother and the child occupied with each other, it couldn't hurt anyone.

Best of all, it kept the child out of Abigail's hair when she came home from school. They hadn't been close, on Abigail's part, since her granddaughter had refused to confide in her about the deer or anything else in her world of play. The tension between them became worse after Edward left for the army. The child took mostly to herself with her bears and her animal friends. It was as though she didn't need her grandmother to occupy her time. They didn't bake together much anymore. Ever since the child stopped talking, Abigail didn't try to communicate with her. It never occurred to Abigail that Gem hadn't lost her hearing and could listen to stories, which she loved to hear from anyone; stories about animals and fairy tales and what lay outside the walls of her "castle". Grand Abbey couldn't be bothered with such foolishness as fairy tales. Life was hard. The sooner the child learned that lesson, the better. Let them pretend that everything was normal at school, but not at home where hard working people did without. On the few occasions that Abigail had taken Gem with her to the market, she was embarrassed how neighbors and women from church avoided running into her and the child. You couldn't talk to a child who cowered behind her like she did and wouldn't respond to their questions. Not so much as a "thank you." No, Abigail told Fred, twice had been enough of an embarrassment. The child was better off at home.

Before Melanie began working at home, Gem's time after school was spent quietly in the backyard while Abigail prepared the meals and knitted or quilted for her church.

The shopping, which would have been an outing for Gem, was managed when the child was in school or when Fred had the time to watch her, or when she napped.

Once, in an angry moment when Gem ignored her warning about going to the back fence where that "louse infested animal pawed the ground," Abbey confessed to Fred that she thought the child was faking. "I've seen her with her bears," she said one evening when she thought they were alone. Melanie was working late in her studio. Abigail and Fred were sitting in the den. "Her lips are moving as she reads them stories," Abigail said to Fred in a whisper as her knitting needles clacked away furiously. "I know she's talking to them. Not to me. Oh, no. She doesn't say one word to me all day long. I am in this house alone with her while you're out in the shed listening to your radio. I have no one to talk to in this house, but there she is talking to her ratty old stuffed bears. It's disrespectful, against the Fifth Commandment. She wouldn't treat me that way if her father were here."

On that occasion, as on many occasions when her grandmother didn't know that she was sitting in the dark at the top of the steps listening, Gem overheard them whispering. She had acute hearing. Nothing much went on in the house or outdoors that she did not overhear. She knew exactly what her grandmother said about her, even under her breath when Gem was supposedly drawing in the other room. Exactly what she said.

Melanie did not share her mother-in-law's thinking that the comics she spent hours drawing were nonsense. They were another art form, she told herself. However, they wouldn't pay the bills if no one saw them. So, one morning after Gem had been picked up by the special bus for school, Melanie put on a suit, which she thought made her look professional, modestly high heels, and a hat. She carefully packaged the first few strips of *Warrior Woman* into a packing carton and headed off in Fred's car for the local paper.

The editor was not available. Could she wait? The receptionist eyed Melanie suspiciously. "Do I know you?" she said.

"I don't think so."

"You look familiar. Wait a minute... are you that woman who painted those pictures on the planes?"

Melanie was shocked that she would be recognized for her paintings. "I am," she admitted. "Where did you-?"

"It's been in all the papers, even the nationals. Wait just a minute." And she disappeared into the back office.

In no time at all a man came out with the

receptionist. He held out his hand and introduced himself. "I'm Harry Meyers, Miss…"

"Mrs. Commons." Melanie shook his hand.

"Commons, that's it. I knew I'd recognize it when I heard it. Come back to my office. Can we get you anything?"

"No, thank you." Melanie guessed that the man was available after all. There was no one in his office.

"Sit down. Sit down. I had the pleasure of being at the unveiling of the P40 when you were honored. We were introduced at the time, but there were so many dignitaries there that morning, it's not surprising you wouldn't remember me."

"I'm sorry."

"No, no. I'm delighted to see you again. What may I do for you?"

"I've turned my hand to comic strip art," Melanie said, saying what she rehearsed. Comic strip art had a more professional sound to it, she thought. Even Marty and Tony told her to call it that when they learned that she had picked up on their idea.

She had yet to tell them about *Warrior Woman,* but planned to do so if there was any acceptance of her work. Or maybe it's just so ridiculous, she thought, like her mother-in-law said.

"Comic strip," Mr. Meyers' eyebrows furrowed. "We're syndicated. Our comics come out of New York, but let's see what you have here."

Melanie took the sketchpad from the carton. She had drawn in the colors of *Warrior Woman's* costume, but everything else was in black and white.

"By jove," Mr. Meyers said in that strange accent, "I think you've got something here."

"Really?"

"Absolutely. Of course, I haven't the authority to publish it, but I can pass it along to the syndicate and see what they think. Are you available to go to New York if they want to talk to you?"

"New York?" Melanie had not been out of Ohio in her twenty eight years. "I…"

"They'd be the ones to decide. I can see a feature article in our own paper, 'local celebrity makes her comic strip debut' sort of thing." He looked down again at the book in his hand. "Personally, I think these are really good. I'm a fan of the comics myself. You in this alone?"

"Pardon me?"

"You write the script as well as the ink."

By "the ink", Melanie assumed that he meant the

drawing. "Yes," she said. "There are no end of stories about rescues."

"That's true, isn't it. Well, leave this with me. I'll have my secretary draft a letter which we'll both sign that I've accepted this submission on behalf of the Hearst Papers. It's standard procedure."

And so, to celebrate, Melanie stopped at the drugstore that morning and had a vanilla phosphate. She stopped by the bakery which she hadn't visited since the letter arrived.

Missing.

Something she'd said in the interview with Mr. Meyers came back to her as she hugged the bakery owner and cried with him. "No end of stories about rescues." If only that were true for Edward.

The time it took for a response from New York dragged by slowly. Melanie continued to turn out her strips, becoming more engaged with her character and the times and places in which she existed. It was war time, when less of everything was the norm, less gas, less meat, less fuel, rationing, families being separated, servicemen *missing*. It wasn't a particularly funny comic, but it was timely and patriotic. And it was based upon every day events surrounding her.

One early evening almost a week later, the phone rang. It was for Melanie. Long distance. For a few seconds, Melanie stopped breathing. *Not... Please not...*

"Mrs. Commons?"

Barely, "Yes."

"This is Foster Willis of the Hearsts Papers. How are you this evening?"

The Hearst Papers. Not the government calling. Not the state department. Not the *bad* news. "Fine, thank you," Melanie lied. Honestly, she would tell Abigail and Fred later, she had no idea who this was calling. It didn't dawn on her.

"We have your comic strip, *Warrior Woman*. It's very clever indeed. I'm familiar with your nose art, Mrs. Commons. Our papers have been full of it for the past year."

Melanie didn't know what to say. "I'm... thank you."

"Could you come to New York? We'd like to talk to you about publishing your comics."

"Come to New York?"

"Yes, ma'am. At our expense, of course. We'll authorize a first class ticket. Would Monday morning be all right with you?"

It was Saturday. Monday. Two days. Melanie glanced at Abigail who was waiting to hear about the call. "I guess I can."

"Good. A courier will be coming by with your ticket. I assume you would fly out of Cleveland."

Melanie had never even been to Cleveland, a hundred or so miles away.

"If you need a ride to the airport..."

"I guess I can get there. What time Monday?"

"It's an early flight. How about this: I'll have a driver pick you up at six a.m. Monday morning and drive you to the airport. It should be about a two hour drive which will get you there in plenty of time for your ten o'clock flight. How does that sound? And, of course, we'll make similar arrangements on your return."

"That would be... grand," Melanie said. Unbelievable.

"One thing, Mrs. Commons, you might give some thought between now and Monday when we meet here at our offices, would you be willing to bring your... what is it you call her...?"

"*Warrior Woman.*"

"Yes, Warrior Woman. Would you be willing to write stories about her in a future world?"

Melanie really didn't understand. It was all so much to absorb. Her thoughts were spinning about luggage, what she would wear, what about Gem, what about...

"We envison *Warrior Woman* existing in a 21st Century," Mr. Willis went on. "You can go wild with what the 21st Century may be like. Perhaps spaceships to the moon."

The most ridiculous thing Melanie ever heard.

"Anyway, think about it. The concept is really quite fun. We are definitely interested."

There was an awkward silence when Melanie repeated once again, "Thank you."

"If there's nothing else, our driver will be at your house Monday morning at 6 a.m. Let me give you my home telephone number in case anything comes up over the week-end. It's 212-731-7077."

Melanie quickly jotted down the number. When she finally found her voice and once again thanked Mr. Willis, the phone went dead.

"What is it?" Abigail asked impatiently.

"The Hearst Papers," Melanie said mechanically. "They want me to come to New York. Monday."

Communion

Chapter Seven

It was no use even trying to explain to Gem about New York. Fred thought he was doing a good thing by getting out the atlas and showing the child New York City on the map. He made the mistake of showing her Cleveland where her mother would be taking off in the plane and New York City where she would be landing. Gem traced the distance with her finger and cried.

"It's perfectly safe, sweetheart," Melanie (who didn't believe a word of it having watched the assembly of military planes) said, trying to console her daughter. "And mommy will be home in two or three days." She hadn't really cleared that with Mr. Willis. He hadn't mentioned the return date, only that they would be handling it at their end.

Abigail was torn between needing the money that steady employment would bring in and worrying that this trip to New York might be a move in that direction.

She thought about Edward coming home and his family gone. Always her thoughts were about her son. It was not ever beyond probability that Edward would one day walk down that lane and knock on their door. Every single time there was a knock on their door, Abigail's heart jumped. Could it be-? What if Edward found his way home only to discover his wife and little girl had gone off to live in a city a thousand miles away.

"You won't be staying?" Abigail said as she helped Melanie pack. Fred had gone into the attic and brought down an old suitcase which had seen better days.

"No, of course, not," Melanie said. "Staying? In New York? Oh, Abigail, this is our home, Gem's and mine."

"And Edward's."

Melanie flinched. "Of course, Edward's." Seeing the tears in her mother-in-law's eyes and for the first time ever realizing the depth of her sorrow, Melanie reached out to embrace Abigail. The woman allowed the younger woman to embrace her. Fred nearly dropped the suitcase as he started to walk into the room and backed out slowly.

Monday morning everyone was up and waiting on the front porch for the driver. Melanie was anxious. Gem was trying very hard not to cry. Abigail and Fred were fidgety. When the big black car approached, Gem started crying. The driver got out of the car at the curb and walked up to take Melanie's suitcase.

Through the back window of the car Melanie watched as her family disappeared in the early morning first light. Fred took Gem, who had given in to near hysterics, inside the house. Abigail remained outside to pull weeds.

It was several miles out of town before the driver dared speak. "Nice day for flying," he said cautiously. Melanie remained quiet. Inside her purse were her drawing pens, black for the outline, red, white and blue for the costume, a small notepad and photos of her nose art. The evening before she called Tony and Marty and told each of them what was happening with her comic strip. They were beside themselves with excitement.

"You need a lawyer," Marty said. "Don't sign anything until you check with a lawyer." It didn't sound like bad advice.

"The 21st century," Tony said. "Wow! Marty and I'll think about that…"

Melanie told them that while they were talking on the phone, Gem was sitting on the floor drawing in her own little notebook. She made a simple drawing of a dog in a costume and it wasn't bad.

"Wonder dog," Marty said. Melanie laughed but it wasn't beyond possibility. After all, she thought, in the 21st Century, anything was possible. Who, in 1944, could say that it wasn't.

Anything was possible, Melanie thought, except what awaited her as she was driven into New York City by a driver who had been waiting at the luggage pickup station with a sign decorated with her name. Never in her life had Melanie seen a building taller than six stories. From a distance, she got her first glimpse of skyscrapers upon her arrival in Cleveland, but not until she rode into the heart of downtown Manhattan, did she realize how high in the sky these buildings soared. She got out of the taxi in front of one of the largest buildings in the city and timidly walked inside carrying her cardboard suitcase.

Chapter Eight

Gem refused to eat that day. She even refused to go with Fred for ice cream. Most of the day she sat with her bears in the bear house and cried.

About eight o'clock that evening, Fred went up to her room to kiss her goodnight. She was in bed asleep, or so Fred thought. He tiptoed over to the bed, bent over her little delicate face, and tenderly kissed Gem's cheek. Then, he tiptoed out of her room again, quietly moving from step to step having memorized all of the stairway's groans.

"She's sound asleep," he told Abigail downstairs. As usual, Abigail was knitting, rocking furiously in her chair.

"She hasn't had anything to eat all day," Fred said.

"She'll eat tomorrow. Don't be fooled by her. She probably has candy bars stashed in her room."

"Don't you know?"

Abigail put down her needles and glared at Fred. "Me? You think she'd let *me* tidy her room? Oh, no, only her mother is allowed in her room. I go in from time to time when she's in school and her mother's out just to see what's so secret up there. I've found candy once or twice. It wouldn't surprise me that she has some of that candy left over from Halloween."

Before Abigail had begun her tirade about Gem's room, Fred picked up the evening paper and was reading it. With Fred's hearing not as sharp as it once was and Abigail's squeaky rocker compounded with the clacking of her needles, neither one of them heard the bedroom door open upstairs. Gem came out quietly and sat in the dark on the landing.

Fred said, "You read this article about that General who lives on the other side of the lake?"

Abigail didn't answer.

"I said, did you-"

"I heard you. When have I had time to read the paper today?"

"It says here that Brigadier General Charles

88

O'Brien, U.S. Army Retired, has moved into the Walker house on the north side of the lake."

"Alone? In that big house?"

"Doesn't say anything about family. He's pretty famous, I guess. Head... Emer...ee.. tus, whatever that is, of Life Magazine."

"Retired."

"Hopes to fish and hunt, it says. Looks like we got us a famous citizen in our little town."

Abigail kept rocking and knitting away, completely absorbed in her own thoughts, uninterested in what Fred found so fascinating about some old General moving into town. But the little girl at the top of the stairs heard every word. At ten o'clock, when the downstairs had been dark for half an hour, Gem crept downstairs and picked up the paper her grandfather had left on the floor beside the divan.

Upstairs in her room, Gem read every word. She was a very good reader, having taught herself even before she learned her letters at school. "A former General in the United States Army," the paper said. "In the army," Gem whispered. Like her daddy. Somebody from the Army who might know something about soldiers who were *missing*.

It was a cold night, below freezing, but that didn't bother Gem. She picked up her letter and the picture of her father that she kept beside her bed, stuffed them into the pocket of her coat, pulled on her leggings and carried her boots so she could walk down the stairs and through the kitchen in her stockings without being heard.

The lock on the back door was too high to reach. As quietly as she could, Gem carried a chair to the door, stood on the chair, and slid the bolt across the frame. Then, she climbed back down, very carefully moved the chair away from the door, opened the door, and backed out as quietly as possible, closing the door behind her without making a sound. She listened as she stood outside in the doorway for any sound from her grandparent's bedroom on the ground floor, but all she heard was her grandfather snoring.

There was a nearly full moon and stars to guide Gem across the back yard and into the field beyond. She put on her boots, climbed the fence as she knew she could, although she had never before tried, and as noiselessly as possible dropped on the other side. She waited to be sure she had not been heard. When no sound of alarm came from the house, Gem slipped away, her only companion the young deer that came up beside her and followed her through the tall brush.

Even if either of Gem's grandparents had awakened and looked outside, they would not have seen their granddaughter making her way across the marshes beside the lake, even in the moonlight. The weeds were as high as the child, hiding her from observation by anyone who lived adjacent to the lake.

There were no lights on in any of the houses, but the moon and the stars were enough light for Gem to see across the lake and to make her path around it, stopping several times to rest. She wasn't afraid even though there were noises she had never heard before. One, an owl she imagined, hooted nearby, but the deer wasn't alarmed and so Gem walked on unafraid. When she rested, the deer rested. Actually, the doe came up to her and put her head in Gem's lap, the animal's big dark eyes shining in the night, when the child sat down in the brush. If she hurried she imagined that she could make it to the big house on the lake, the one that had always been known as the "Walker House" because the Walker family had lived there for years until Mr. Walker passed away not long ago and the property sold.

Gem could see the Walker house in the distance. Because she was keeping her eye on the house, she stumbled more than once, falling in the wet marsh near the lake, dirtying her leggings and coat, but she didn't care. She kept on walking.

Gem couldn't know that on that particular morning, General O'Brien had planned a fishing trip downstream before sunrise, the best time to fish. It was nearly three o'clock in the morning when he began hauling out his fishing tackle, rods and reel, a thermos of coffee and a basket of sandwiches. He made several trips, nearly ready to shove off when he heard a rustle in the brush alongside his property.

Fortunately for Gem and the small deer accompanying her, General O'Brien had planned a fishing trip, not a hunting trip, on that morning and he was not armed as he would have been if it were ducks he was after instead of trout.

The first thing the General could make out was a small deer who appeared at the edge of the tall brush. The deer stood brazenly looking at General O'Brien. As the General was about to shove his boat into the water, the deer moved aside and a very dirty little girl appeared behind the deer.

General O'Brien stopped in his tracks. "What-?"

Without a word, the little girl sloshed her way up to the General, her leggings muddy and soaked. Her coat was filthy; her nose was red; she wore neither a hat nor mittens, though it was below forty degrees that morning.

Before the General could speak, the little girl came up to him and started to cry. She seemed to be trying to speak, but nothing came out. Just before she fell on the ground, the General reached out and grabbed her.

Communion

Chapter Nine

Abigail awakened as usual that morning, dressing quickly and turning on the light in the kitchen to start the morning's breakfast. There was nobody who had to be up at that hour, not Edward or Melanie and certainly not Fred any longer, but it was her habit and habits were hard to break. It was almost five o'clock, barely light when she reached for the coffee. One of the kitchen chairs was out of place. Fred, again, she thought angrily. What if she'd come into the kitchen to get a drink of water in the middle of the night and fallen over the chair? She and Fred would have words about this when the inconsiderate man showed his face for breakfast some time later.

The kitchen was ice cold. Abigail started the stove and the oven and the small heater she used to heat that part of the house. No sense in turning on the furnace to heat the rest of the house, she always said, when all they used most of the day, especially the winter days, was the kitchen.

She started the coffee, took some eggs out for frying and batter to make pancakes, bread for toast, some butter and jam because the child would be hungry that morning having gone to bed without supper.

She was just bending over to light the oven, which had to be lit with a match, when she thought she heard a knock on the front door.

"Now who," she thought, "at this hour-" She opened the hall door leading to the entry and peeked out the glass window of the front door.

A man in a woolen hat and what appeared to be hunting clothes was standing at their door. Abigail was not about to open up for a stranger calling no matter what time it was. "What do you want?" she said, reaching for an umbrella in the stand next to the door in case the man tried to get in.

"I'm General O'Brien," the man said. "I have your... granddaughter, I guess she is."

With that, Abigail looked down for the first time

and saw a dirty, muddy, tear stained girl on the porch beside the man. At first, in the dim light, Abigail did not recognize her own granddaughter.

"What is it?" Fred said, coming into the hall, pulling up his suspenders.

Abigail opened the door. Gem cowered behind the man in the hunting attire.

"She's frozen to the core," the man said. "She needs thawing out."

Fred stepped in front of Abigail who seemed glued to the spot. He picked up Gem, mud and all and carried her into the house.

"Where did you- How-" Abigail started to say.

"She was in the brush by the lake."

"What brush?"

"In the back of my house."

"*Your house?* You mean the Walker house. On the other side of the lake?"

"I'm afraid so." The General's tone was not friendly. Fred had grabbed a blanket off the divan and wrapped it around Gem. He returned to the open door with the child wrapped in the blanket in his arms.

"Come in," Fred said. "Abbey, where's your manners. Open the door and let the General in."

"I'd like to talk to you," the General said, walking through.

"I don't understand," Abigail repeated more than once.

"Make some coffee, Abbey. Come in. Come in." Fred continued to hold Gem in his arms.

"You might want to start a warm bath for the child," the General suggested. "I'm sure she's wet to the core and freezing."

Abigail held out her arms, but Gem clung to her grandfather.

"I'll take care of it," Fred said and he walked to the back room with his granddaughter.

General O'Brien stood his ground. He was not about to leave without hearing the story of why and how this couple's granddaughter came to locate him. Abigail seemed reluctant to ask him to come in, but he was in and she had no recourse.

"I was just making coffee," she said. "Come into the kitchen where it's warm."

The General followed her. The coffee was ready and she poured a cup.

"Thanks," the General said and sat down at the table.

"I don't understand," Abigail repeated again.

"I don't either," the General said. "Why was the child running away?"

Abigail gasped. "Running away? Of course, she didn't run away."

"From your house to my house, through the brush at night, I'd say took about five hours on foot, a child's footing. She did have one companion, a small deer that appeared to be with her."

"A…?"

"You weren't aware that she left the house?"

"Of course not. You think I'd be going about my business of making breakfast if I had any idea that she was out there."

"That's what I'm asking," the General said. "She came to see me especially. She knew where I lived."

"How?" And then Abigail recalled the conversation of the evening before when Fred read from the paper about a General in the United States Army moving into the Walker house.

"She gave me this," General O'Brien said. He took an envelope out of his jacket pocket and handed it to Abigail.

"What is it?"

'It's a letter. I'm guessing it's from her father. Somewhere in Germany. The address on the front of the envelope is how I found this house."

"What was she doing with this?"

"I can only guess that she thought I might be able to find him. She didn't say anything. Her teeth were chattering so, she couldn't speak. But, I heard her say, 'Missing'. I didn't misunderstand that. Is this so?"

"She spoke? She doesn't speak. More than three years now. Ever since my son's been missing in action. My son, Edward, is the child's father. I presume she thought that you being a five star general…"

"One star. Brigadier."

Abigail shrugged. It made no difference to her. "That you might be able to find her father. The foolish girl."

"Not so foolish. Very brave, I'd say, to walk out into the night through scary woods and freezing temperature. Very brave, indeed."

Abigail backed off. "Well, of course, it was brave, but still a foolish thing to do. If she wanted to visit you, she should have told us in the morning and, of course, we would have taken her to call on you."

"Where is her mother?"

Abigail snorted. It was her one chance to redeem

herself. She was not a bad grandmother. It was her mother who had left the child to traipse off to the big city after a pipedream. "She's gone to New York."

"She lives here with you?"

"Yes."

"And you and your husband were supposed to be watching..."

"Not 'supposed to be.' We were watching her."

The General stared at Abigail, making her flinch.

"She stormed up to her room last night and wouldn't eat her dinner. Fred checked on her later and said she was sound asleep. I decided not to bother her."

"And not to check on her either."

Abigail glared at him. General or not, he couldn't talk that way to her. She was not one of his enlisted men he could order around.

"When will her mother return?" the General asked.

"We don't know." Abigail was cool now, after the shock of seeing Gem at the door when she was presumed to be upstairs in her bed. Abigail now turned belligerent that this person should stand there and accuse her of being negligent.

General O'Brien stood. "I'll call back later after the child has had a good sleep and something to eat. Please call the mother and inform her as to what's happened. I'll want to speak to her when she returns."

Orders. Orders! Abigail was just about to tell the pompous General looking down on her now to go jump in a lake when he suddenly turned abruptly and walked out of the house to his car at the curb. *Who did he think he was? Patton?*

Chapter Ten

Fred wanted to call Melanie immediately and tell her what happened, but Abigail reminded him that they had no way to reach her and besides, the child was safe. Her mother could be told when she returned home, whenever that might be.

As fortune would have it, Melanie called home that very evening. Fred wanted Abigail to tell her then, but Abigail shook her head while she told Melanie that everything was just fine. "When you coming home?" she asked.

"Tomorrow," Melanie said. "I signed the contract today. I meet with the publishers again tomorrow morning and then they'll take me to the airport. Is Gem all right?"

Fred had his ear to the phone as well. Abigail put a finger to her mouth and gave him a threatening look.

"She's fine," Abigail said. "We'll see you tomorrow."

After she hung up, Fred shook his head and his finger at her. "You should have told her."

"There's time. The child's fine. Maybe it would be best if we don't tell her mother at all."

"Abigail! What if that General fellow comes back here?"

That was a problem…

"I'll take care of him," Abigail parried.

Fred didn't doubt for a second that she could take care of anyone, but he said with as much of an opposite position as he'd ever taken against his wife, "You don't want him going to the authorities. If Melanie finds out from somebody else, she may take the child away, go live on their own, maybe in that New York City. Then, if Edward comes home…"

"Don't say 'if'. Don't ever say 'if'."

"Okay, then: *when* Edward comes home, he'll join her up there and we'll never see them again."

Abigail's back straightened, her mouth set, lips twitched. She knew Fred was right this time. She couldn't lose her son again. "I'll tell her," she said finally. "Don't say a word when she comes in. I'll tell her."

But, of course, when Melanie arrived the next afternoon in the same car that took her away, with the same driver, Gem rushed out into her arms and Fred said, "She's okay now that you're home."

Abigail glared, *glared* at him.

Melanie invited the driver in for a cup of coffee, but he declined. He tipped his chauffer's hat to Abigail and Fred after he carried Melanie's suitcase onto the front porch. "Good afternoon, Princess," he said to Gem, who looked frightened of him as she clung with her arms around her mother's neck, her cheeks pressed to hers.

Even before the car had pulled away, Melanie asked, "What's wrong with Gem?"

"Get inside," Abigail said, "before the nosy neighbors come out and want to know all about that car."

They went inside. Fred took Melanie's suitcase upstairs. Before he reached the upstairs landing, Melanie asked again, "What's wrong with Gem?" The child continued to cling to her refusing to be put down.

"It's okay, sweetheart," Melanie said. "What is it, Abigail?"

"I think it's better we talk after. Put her down."

But Gem would not let go. "Tell me now," Melanie said.

Fred remained at the top of the stairs as Abigail started in. "She went for a walk," she said, making it sound all perfectly innocent, as if her granddaughter always went for a walk by herself.

"You mean..." Melanie tried once again to put her down. "Let me sit down, sweetheart," she said finally. She carried Gem with her to the sofa and the two of them sat with Gem in her arms, the back of her head facing her grandmother in the rocker opposite the sofa. "When was this?" Melanie asked. She couldn't know that her question was the key to the problem. It thwarted Abigail's plan to tell the story before she had to mention that it was the middle of the night when Gem left the house for a walk through the woods.

"After we went to sleep," Abigail said suddenly. Fred sat down on the top step to listen and wait for Melanie's reaction.

"What? At night? She went for a walk at night?"

Melanie felt the child in her arms shaking. "It's okay, sweetheart," she said reassuringly. "It's okay. I just want to hear the story. Mommy isn't mad. Just let me..."

"Snuck out," Abigail said derisively. She got that in

before going on with the story. "We woke up the next morning…"

"She was outside the entire night and you didn't know?"

"I just told you. She *snuck* out the back door. Fred was snoring away. I can't hear anything over his snoring. I was exhausted from watching her all day and by the time I laid…"

"Just go on, Abbey. You didn't realize she was gone until when…"

"I was just about to go up and wake her. I waited a bit thinking if she was as tired and worn out as I was, she'd need her sleep."

"Abbey… please."

"And the doorbell rang."

"She rang the doorbell?"

"No. Some retired Major General or something was with her."

"*Oh my God!*"

"He just moved in. He saw the child out walking and brought her home."

Melanie shifted her daughter in her arms. She checked to see if she was crying, then turned back to Abigail. "How did he know where she lived?"

"She had a letter with her. She stole the letter from your room."

Upstairs, Fred shook his head. "Make her out a thief *and* a runaway."

"What letter?"

"One of Edward's. Go get that letter, Gem Marie."

"No, no," Melanie said quickly. "I'll see it later. So, she had a letter addressed to me with our address. And this Major General-"

Fred said "Brigadier General" quietly. He wanted to scream it. He wanted to scream, period.

"That's what they're saying," Abigail reported.

"Who's saying?"

"The papers. This retired General's moved into the old Walker house. He found her."

"The *Walker House*. On the other side of the lake? She walked around the lake?" Melanie looked at her daughter who would not lift her head from her mother's jacket.

"I don't know exactly where he found her. But, he had the good sense to bring her home. I hate to think what the neighbors would say if the police brought her home, running out of here like that in the middle of the night. Shame on you."

Melanie patted her daughter's back. "But, why?" she asked Abigail.

"Why what?"

"Why did she run away?"

"She wasn't running away. She's happy here... with me and Fred. She evidently got it in her fool head that this general could find her daddy, I'm thinking. So, she stole that letter out of your room and decided on her own to go find him. I saw the newspaper with the article about that General moving into the Walker house on her bed when I went up later to give her a warm bath and put her down."

Again, at the top of the stairs, Fred could hardly contain himself. _She gave her a bath? She put her down?_

Melanie rocked the child in her arms. Her body was tense and shaking as she cried softly. "Let's go upstairs," Melanie said. "Come along with mommy."

They left the parlor. Fred came down the steps to help her. He took Gem from Melanie and carried her up the stairs to her room.

Downstairs, Abigail called up, "Wash up while you're up there. Dinner's almost ready."

But Melanie was too upset to even answer Abigail. She didn't for a minute believe the story she just heard. It was too "her side of it". Who could tell the other side?

"May I borrow your car, Fred?"

Fred, understanding all too well what his daughter-in-law was planning, nodded, hugged and kissed his granddaughter in his arms. Melanie reached for Gem.

"We'll go together."

Chapter Eleven

The trees around the Walker house were bare. It was just beginning to snow. To somehow make it fun and divert her daughter's attention as they walked up the dirt path to the mansion, Melanie leaned back, opened her mouth, and tried to catch snowflakes. After a few attempts, her daughter, walking beside her clutching her hand, did the same. By the time they reached the big house with the stone dogs on either side of the door, Gem was too busy catching snowflakes to be anxious when Melanie pushed the doorbell.

It took only a few seconds for someone to answer. A large woman in a long white apron opened the door.

"I'm Melanie Commons," Melanie said. "This is my daughter, Gem. Is the Major General at home?"

A booming voice behind the woman in the apron said, "I've been promoted and not even a soldier any more. Hello there." A man as big as his voice came around to greet them. "Here's my little friend."

Melanie thought that Gem would immediately cower behind her, but surprisingly she stepped in front of her mother and held out her hand to the man, which he took in both of his and shook and shook and shook. "You're all cleaned up," he said. "I didn't know you were so beautiful." He touched the top of her head. "And you must be momma."

Melanie shook hands as well. "I've come-" she started to say.

"Come in. Where's my hospitality? Margaret, see if we have any of those biscuits you make for our tea. Margaret runs this house. I just live here." He held the door open wide. Gem walked in without any prodding from her mother, like she'd been there before. And perhaps she had, Melanie thought. She knew she hadn't heard all of the story of her visit yet.

"I don't see your little friend," the General said as he looked outside before closing the door.

"Her little friend?" Melanie said.

"A doe. About the size of her. She was with... I don't even know her name."

"It's Gem, short for Gemini."

"Gem. You are that, my dear. Let me take your coat."

Gem dutifully unbuttoned her coat and allowed the General to help her out of it. The General then did the same for Melanie.

"It's so good of you to see us," Melanie said. "I hope we're not interfering with your dinner."

"Dinner? Won't eat for hours. Haven't had our tea yet, have we Margaret?" He called that last to Margaret, somewhere in the house, probably the kitchen, Melanie supposed. "Come into the kitchen. We've got the stove going in there. Otherwise, the house is a tomb, cold as..." Melanie thought that the man was going to say something that he realized was better left unsaid. "Cold as an icicle hanging from your nose. How's that?" He touched Gem's nose. "In here," he said, opening a swinging door to a very large room with a pot bellied stove, all nice and cozy, two rocking chairs in front of the stove, and a divan, a hooked rug and behind this setting a wonderful old but inviting kitchen with a round table and four chairs. Newspapers were piled high on one of the rocking chairs. "Here let me move those papers," the General said, picking up the papers and putting them on the floor. "Now, make yourself comfortable. Best room in the house. Couldn't keep up the place without Margaret. Been with me for years. You like it here better than Washington, don't you, Margaret?"

"I do, indeed, General. How do you take your tea, Missus?"

"Plain, thank you. It's a lovely room." There was a big cat napping on the brick shelf about a foot off the floor beside the stove, where it was warm. Gem immediately walked over to pet the cat.

"Gem-" her mother started to warn her.

"It's all right," the General said. "The cat loves to be loved. Don't we all? Margaret, I think one of your famous hot chocolates with lots of whipping cream might tickle the little angel here." Gem was too busy picking up the cat and petting it to hear.

"Sit down, sit down," the General insisted. "I understand that your husband is overseas."

"Missing," Melanie said. She never said that word but that she practically choked on it. It usually came out like a hiss.

"Missing, is he? I didn't know that."

"Can you tell me about that evening that you found Gem?"

"I found...? I think it's the other way around, Mrs. Commons."

"Please, Melanie."

"Thank you. Such pretty names in your family. As I said, it was the other way around. Your little girl found me. And lucky she came by when she did. I was just getting ready to shove off to go fishing."

"I can't believe that she walked all the way from our house to here," Melanie said. "She could have been hit by a car out on the road, or picked up by anyone." Melanie shuddered saying it out loud.

"Oh, she wasn't on the road," General O'Brien said. "She came through the brush and if you'd seen the likes of her all muddied and exhausted, you'd have wondered how she made her way through all that weed. I have to get the county or whoever's responsible to do something about that before next spring. It's a fire hazard."

"She made her way through the woods without getting lost?"

"She had a guide. The doe I mentioned. That doe was walking ahead of her and I believe she made sure that your little girl found where she was going. Young animals and young humans have a special bond. I'm sure of that."

"Incredible."

"It was heartbreaking. That's what it was. Your little girl wants her daddy home. When she handed me that letter and stood there waiting for me to do something about it, I almost broke down myself. Has she been mute since birth?"

"No," Melanie said. "It happened suddenly, one morning while she was in the kitchen with my mother-in-law. She grabbed her chest like she had some sort of seizure or something and she hasn't uttered a word since. We've had her to all kinds of doctors. They can't find any reason why she stopped talking. No physical reason, anyway."

The General sat back and rocked. "Were you there when it happened?"

"No. I was at work. At that time, my husband was overseas."

"Anyone else with her besides your mother-in-law?"

Melanie thought for a second. "No," she said. "I heard what happened from Abigail, my mother-in-law, when I got home."

The General didn't say anything. Just rocked.

Margaret served the tea, biscuits, and hot chocolate. Gem put the cat down, sat on the brick shelf with her cup of cocoa and ate two biscuits.

"Is there anything else I should know," Melanie said, "about that night?"

"Morning," General O'Brien corrected her. "Almost four a.m. After I read the letter, I told her I'd take her home. I have to say, Mrs.... Melanie, she didn't want to go. I felt like she wanted me to do something. I guess about the letter."

"Abigail told me a little while ago when I got home that Gem had evidently read about you in the newspaper. That section of the paper was up in her room. She's a very good reader. When she read you were in the army, my guess is she thought you might be able to find her father. I can't think of any other explanation for her coming to see you."

"And she couldn't tell anyone why she wanted to visit me."

"No. Unfortunately, not. But when I think of what might have happened to her out there alone."

"Not alone," the General said. "She was definitely not alone."

"That little doe you mentioned wouldn't have been much help."

"That little doe has a mother and father somewhere

nearby, don't you think?"

It wasn't until then that Melanie suddenly remembered the story that Abigail told her some time back about the deer in the back of the house, how Gem appeared to be talking to it. "There have been incidents," Melanie admitted. "There's a deer beyond the gate at the house. Gem has been seen out at the back fence next to it. At first, I was alarmed, but my father-in-law told me that the deer is harmless. The two of them—Gem and the deer—seem to enjoy each other's company."

"And communicate," General O'Brien said. "You do believe that humans communicate with animals?"

Melanie smiled. No, she didn't, but there were definitely some signs in her young daughter's life that she and animals had some bond or other between them. If what the General said about the deer leading Gem through the brush at night was true, yes, she would now believe that humans and animals were able to communicate with each other.

She looked over at Gem and the cat that was resting with its head in her lap while she nibbled at a biscuit.

"Now let's talk about your husband," General O'Brien said, setting down his tea on the small table between the rockers. "When were you informed that he's missing?"

"Two years this June. The twenty third to be exact." The General rocked. He picked up a pipe off the table and put it in his mouth.

"I don't smoke any more," he said to Melanie. "I just like the feel of the pipe when I'm thinking." And he thought and he rocked while the clock in the kitchen ticked loudly, the cat purred and Gem and Melanie watched.

"I assume you've saved his letters," he said finally.

"Every one."

"I'd like to see them. I need to know his rank and anything else we can learn from the letters that may give us some hint about where he was."

"They were postmarked Germany."

"That could be true or not. If he was behind enemy lines, as I assume he was, they were probably on the move. You have no objection to my reading the letters?"

"None whatsoever."

"Good. I'm not sure I can do anything, but I can at least look into it."

Melanie stood. "I can't tell you how grateful we'd be."

General O'Brien nodded toward Gem and the cat. "She can't tell me either, but I know how grateful she'd be. I don't want to make her any promises I can't deliver, but we'll see. It won't be soon, I warn you. These things take way too much time. Lots of red tape before you get to the right department."

"We're just grateful that you'll take the time."

"Time's what I have lots of these days. Right, Margaret?"

"If you say so, General."

"Isn't she wonderful," he said to Melanie. "I'll see you out." Very abrupt. Very business like. Tea time was over.

Before they left the kitchen, both the General and Melanie looked back at Gem and the cat. They were staring at each other, faces close together. Then, Gem got up and walked over to the door to stand beside her mother.

"Thank you for the tea and the hot chocolate," Melanie said.

Gem took the General's hand and kissed it. Melanie had never seen her daughter do that before to anyone.

"There's my thanks," General O'Brien said. "I'm putty in her hands, but don't tell anyone. Generals are supposed to be tough."

Chapter Twelve

It was January when Melanie and Gem visited the General. But, it was April before any real changes were made in Melanie's and Gem's routines. Spring had come to Erieville. Trees were blossoming, birds were nesting, and Gem's garden was ready to plant, all of which kept the little girl occupied while her mother sat in her studio drawing her comic strip.

Success had come to Melanie in the form of a contract beyond the one year she had signed in New York. It arrived in the mail in a large, thick envelope. Twenty two pages of whereases and therefores and parties of the first part and second part until Melanie's head was spinning. She had the good sense to take the contract to a lawyer she'd gone to school with and who now had an office in town. He explained the contract to Melanie, made a few minor suggestions, (probably to earn his fee), but all in all he said it was very advantageous for Melanie to sign it as is before they changed their minds. He congratulated Melanie on such good fortune. She signed, sent a copy back to New York, and settled into a security the young mother hadn't known ever in her life. For the next five years, she would be paid an enormous amount of money every week to draw *Warrior Woman*. If she wanted to draw several weeks ahead, she could even take time off to go somewhere with her daughter, like a vacation, which she never had in her life except for a week-end honeymoon eight years ago.

The little account that Melanie and Edward had established when they got married now had enough money in it for a down payment on a house. Their very own house: hers, Gem's, and Edward's. Melanie dreamed of it so often, could almost draw it the way she saw it, two stories, bedrooms upstairs, big kitchen and family room where she could cook and Edward could bake and still they could be together as a family in the same room, not unlike the General's kitchen. And a studio for Melanie facing the woods, and a big garden for Gem and a real playhouse for her bears; a swing and a slide, a back yard big enough for a picnic table and benches for eating outside in the summer, an apple tree, two apple trees and a white picket fence surrounding the property. It was all so perfect.

On April 3rd, Melanie's dreams for moving into a house with Gem became real in a way she could never have imagined. Melanie had not disclosed the details of her contract with Abigail or Fred. She thought this was between her and Edward some day. It was money to be set aside for their future, especially Gem's future, with special schools most likely for the next ten years or so. She had not paid Fred rent for the rooms upstairs and the sun porch which he had converted for her. Once she started earning money of her own, Melanie had offered to help with the family's finances, but Fred wouldn't hear of it. He said as long as Melanie could afford the schools for Gem, and not seek financial help from them, that she was doing all that she could. Abigail would never dream that Melanie could earn a decent living from her little comics, let alone the amount she received as a signing bonus and the paycheck she would be depositing directly to the bank each month.

The ink on the five year contract was hardly dry before Abigail came home from the market one day and asked Melanie if they could talk.

"Of course," Melanie said. *What's this?* she wondered.

"There's a bulletin board at the market," Abigail began. She was standing in the kitchen, hadn't even put away the groceries before she started in. "You know the one, notices from people looking for work. Well, there's an ad up there asking for rooms to rent. A professor at the college, male, very neat he says, only needs a bedroom and bathroom privileges. Just been hired by the college and looking to move in."

Melanie, having poured herself a cup of tea, had no idea where this was going, but Abigail seemed barely able to hide her excitement about something. "So, I thought maybe you and the child (*will you ever refer to her by her name*) could find a place of your own now that you're working and we could rent out that bedroom we're using and the sun porch and the downstairs bath for a nice little income. We could use the money what with Fred piling up the medical bills, always going off to the doctor for something or other. And my health isn't perfect any more. It's a chore for me to cook for so many extra people in the house now and look after the child while you draw."

Melanie couldn't believe her ears. There were so many falsehoods in that list of reasons why Abigail wanted to do this that Melanie wanted to scream. *Look after 'the child'? When have you looked after 'the child' lately? While I draw?* Abigail would never recognize Melanie's art as anything more than "sitting around drawing those little comics of hers".

Fortunately, Melanie held her tongue. This was exactly what she wanted, to move into their own place. It was a gift that Abigail was practically begging her to accept. She shoved her indignation down as far as it would go, put on her acquiescent, slightly put-out face and said, "If you have an opportunity to bring in some income, Abbey, of course I want you to take it."

"Then it's settled," Abigail said excitedly. "Fred and I have been talking for awhile about taking in boarders. We could rent out the bedroom upstairs. We'll start with just one and see how it goes. I could offer breakfast in the morning to the boarders and if they wanted dinner that would be extra." *What happened to feeling overworked from cooking for extra people in the house?*

Melanie surmised that Fred knew nothing at all about this proposal because even before Abigail put her perishables away, she hurried out to the shed to talk to Fred. *No doubt the first he heard about boarders,* Melanie thought correctly.

But... it was all good news. She put the perishables away, got her coat and proceeded to walk into town so she could think and visit the real estate agent on the square before Abigail changed her mind. She left a note for Abigail that she would be back in a couple of hours, *before* Gem arrived home from school. She wanted to add, so you won't have to take care of "the child", but now was not the time for righteousness. Now was the time to take the bull by the horns and move!

"There's the Cummings house," the Realtor said when Melanie told her what she was looking for in the way of a house for the three of them. "It's only two bedrooms and a convertible den, but it's very sweet."

"Sweet" sounded like run-down to Melanie. She actually knew the house. Every house in town went by the previous owner's name. The Walker house, the Cummings house. She could do better, she thought, than the Cummings house. She knew that she would have to disclose her income on the mortgage application with the bank, but confidentially. "Anything else?" Melanie inquired.

"You *are* looking to rent?" the realtor said. Her name was Mary Jo Williams and she was the only realtor in town, having run off everyone else who tried to sell property. Mary Jo knew everybody in town, and every secret in town which folks were evidently afraid she'd disclose if they even thought of going to someone else for a house. No, Mary Jo was *the* realtor in town. She saw to that.

"Are you still seeing that good looking Mr. Hesseman from the factory?" she asked so non-discreetly. Then, confidentially added, "There's talk about him being a spy."

See, Melanie thought, *every little dirty secret in town.*

She didn't answer. "I'm looking to buy," she said proudly, and Mary Jo suddenly came alive with all kinds of properties for sale. She was now Melanie's best friend... No more talk about beaus at the factory.

There were two houses in Melanie's price range. One was not within walking distance of Abigail. "May we see that one?" Melanie asked.

Mary Jo was all for picking up Melanie and Gem after school, but that wouldn't leave any time for Melanie to talk to Gem about moving, and she didn't want to do it in front of Mary Jo, so Melanie asked if they could make it a little later, say six o'clock. That was all "perfect" with Mary Jo. The house they were going to be looking at was empty.

There was no reason to check in with anyone else. Six o'clock.

On the walk home, Melanie rehearsed what she would tell Abbey and Fred about leaving to see a house. Once they saw Mary Jo Williams, they would know where she and Gem were going. So? Melanie braced herself for the questions and what she would say in response and had all but invented the entire conversation they would have before she opened the front door. All of it unnecessary.

Abigail was buzzing around like a bee. Poor Fred was sitting in the kitchen watching Abbey cleaning out drawers, making lists, talking incessantly.

"There you are," she said when Melanie walked in. "We rented it!"

Fred looked down into his coffee cup.

"To the professor. We decided to give him the upstairs for privacy, you know. You and the child can move in together. He's coming over in a few minutes to see it. Would you make sure that your rooms are picked up?"

Melanie couldn't look at Fred any more than he could look at her. "Of course," she said. "When would he be wanting to move in?"

"Right away. This weekend. And I got an enormous rent, didn't I, Fred. Of course, he'll love it. Such a nice man on the phone. A widower. I threw in breakfast and gave him a very reasonable price on dinner."

Melanie had never seen her mother-in-law so excited, not even when Gem was carried over her threshold. "Congratulations," she said and left, heading upstairs to "pick up," something which she did every morning before leaving hers and Gem's rooms.

In this moment as she climbed the stairs, Melanie realized two things that were true. One, Abigail was convinced that her son was never coming back from the war, and two, her son's wife and daughter were not her responsibility.

Communion

Chapter Thirteen

That afternoon, Melanie invited Fred to go with her and Gem to see the house. She kind of invited Abigail, extending the invitation to everyone in the room, but as she hoped, Abigail was too busy to leave the house. There were linens to change and curtains to hang—the ones she saved for company—and soups to make and sausage to grind and... so many things. "You go, Fred," she said. "I need space."

Melanie was delighted to give Abigail some space. When Mary Jo pulled up in front, Melanie and Fred, swinging Gem between them, piled into the car.

"You know my father-in-law, Fred Commons,"

Melanie said, "and my daughter, Gem."

Obviously, Mary Jo knew all about the Commons' family. She smiled at Gem.

The girl is mute, not deaf, Melanie wanted to say. It was a common mistake when people came up to them in the market or in town. They spoke to Melanie, but would only nod and smile to Gem. As a result, Gem would cower behind her mother shyly. Only Melanie knew that her daughter was not shy. Hadn't she held out her hand and taken the General's hand, practically inviting herself inside.

No matter. Nothing could spoil the elation Melanie felt as they pulled up in front of what she knew when she saw it would be their new home. The house Mary Jo showed them was not exactly Melanie's dream house, but it had several features on the brochure that were exciting. One, a screened-in back porch which ran the width of the house, and two, a picture of a nice size yard with a huge tree for shade and lots of room to rebuild Gem's bear house.

Gem rushed out of the back seat, Fred trailing, up to the front porch. Her hands were together; she was jumping up and down and grinning from ear to ear.

"I think she likes it," Mary Jo said. This was going to be an easy sell, no doubt, for the asking price. However, Fred was quick to point out that the front porch needed some boards replaced and the banister was wobbly and... he went on until both Melanie and Mary Jo tuned him out.

Once inside, Gem raced through the house to the back to stare out at the yard. What the adults heard in the parlor was some kind of ecstatic noise. Gem had figured out how to open the back door and was running around the back yard touching everything, every bush, the tree, the grass, the fence, the hose, the spigot, the cellar door, and then she circled the yard and touched everything again.

"Marking it," Fred said. "It's hers."

Even before we agreed on the cost? Melanie wanted to say, but the cost that Mary Jo had quoted was within her budget. The down payment would be covered by Melanie's signing fee which had already been deposited into the growing bank account of Edward and Melanie Commons.

"Gem, come see the upstairs."

She beat them up the steps, opening doors, looking in, racing to the next door, looking in. She looked at her mother anxiously. Melanie looked over the rooms and then pointed to the one off what was surely the master bedroom. "Yours," she said to the delighted little girl. Gem went into what was now officially her room and closed the door behind her.

"Oh, Good Lord," Melanie said, "I just realized that

we don't have furniture. Not even beds." There was no way she was going to take anything out of Abigail's house, no matter what Fred offered. Abbey would need every stitch of furniture to make her house comfortable for her boarders.

"There's an estate sale this week-end," Mary Jo said. "You could pick up all kinds of furniture there. It's quite lovely for the price."

Back downstairs, Melanie inspected the kitchen. It would need remodeling one day. Not now, but one day. For now, it was adequate. Fred already walked off the area for wainscoating, if Melanie wanted it or paneling or whatever else she wanted.

The garage was attached to the house. "Good," Fred said. "Safer when you come in at night."

"Not that I'll be needing the garage," Melanie said, but maybe some day she and Gem would own a car. Fred had already eyed a space in the garage for a workshop. Plenty of room even with a car.

Back inside, Melanie announced, "We'll take it."

Fred was aghast. "You have to make an offer first."

"It's fairly priced," Melanie said. "I'll be talking to the bank tomorrow."

Of course, Mary Jo was delighted. She was prepared to accept an offer and talk to the owners about a counter offer, then come back to Melanie, and so forth, but Melanie had made her life simple and lucrative. "I'll even throw in a rug for the foyer," she said. "I have one in my attic which will just be perfect for the entry."

They had to pry Gem out of her room. She begged to be able to sleep there that night, but Melanie finally convinced her that the house wasn't theirs yet. However—with a nod from Mary Jo—she jumped the gun and said that it would be by the weekend and then they would begin moving over their things.

Fred asked if he could talk to Melanie privately. Mary Jo went back to the car to get out the paperwork for Melanie to sign.

"Listen, daughter," (as Fred called her when Abigail wasn't around), "I've got some money that Abbey doesn't know about. I can let you have…"

Melanie put her arm around her favorite in-law and kissed him on the cheek. "Thank you, Fred. I will never forget that you offered, but I can afford the down payment and the mortgage. I've already talked to the bank when I deposited a signing bonus that was given to me in New York."

Fred was dumbfounded. He let Melanie kiss him again then stepped out of the way to let her sign here, sign here, sign here, sign here, sign here and sign here as Mary Jo directed her. When it was all done, Melanie, Gem and Fred stood in the front yard looking up at the house. Gem pointed to the porch. A cat that looked for all the world like Muffin, Abigail's cat, was sitting on the banister.

"How in the world...?" Fred said.

Chapter Fourteen

Melanie went to the estate sale alone. She knew that Gem would want to buy everything she saw and there was just so much money to spend on furnishings. The furnishings were fairly priced, being second, or probably third hand, and Melanie found some items that she would have chosen for herself new.

There were two beds, one for each of them, a double for Melanie and a single for Gem, a dresser for each one and a hooked rug similar to the one in General O'Brien's big room. Melanie had hoped to find a table and chairs for the kitchen, but they were taken by the time she arrived at the sale. She did manage to pick up a few dishes, cups and saucers, some mismatched flatware and a tea kettle.

Saturday morning, two men that Mary Jo had hired (and Melanie paid) brought the beds and the dressers and the rugs to the new house. Melanie and Gem were there to meet them. Shortly thereafter, Mary Jo arrived with the signed copies of the agreement to purchase the property. The loan had gone through the bank. Melanie had signed the papers and it was all legal. Their little house was beginning to look lived in and loved.

Fred couldn't get away Saturday, that being the day that the professor was also moving in, but he managed to make two trips with their clothes in the car.

Abigail had thrown in some pots and pans that were tucked away in the cellar and some home made preserves, a crock of pickles and a jar of apple butter.

The evening before, Fred had taken all of the back yard furniture that belonged to his grand-daughter—most of it handmade by Fred himself—and driven it over to the new house. Gem had helped him place the furniture in the back yard, showing her grandpa exactly where each piece was to go. Fred swore later to Melanie that he heard a screech-like sound out of Gem when the bear's house was just the way she wanted it. "Like a giggle, only more delightful. I hope to hear it again," he'd said. "It makes my heart full to see her so happy."

And, who was there to greet Melanie and Gem and Fred and the movers that sunny, wonderful morning but Muffin. "I think he's your cat now," Fred said. "Abbey never took care of him anyway. I'll bring over his food next time."

"I'll get some when we go grocery shopping later," Melanie said. Gem, who had never been allowed to have Muffin inside Abbey's house, picked her up, and carried the cat across the threshold.

"It looks like she's our cat now," Melanie said. She had an arm around Fred as they followed Gem inside.

Sunday morning early, when they least expected it, after both of them spent the first night in Melanie's bed, there was a knock at the door. At barely seven o'clock. Melanie quickly put on a robe, grabbed her slippers, and she and Gem, still in her nightgown, went downstairs to see who it was. "Probably grandpa," Melanie said, but she looked out through the stained glass window and hurried to close her robe before opening the door.

"General O'Brien!"

"Well, here you are. Did you think I wouldn't find you? I was in charge of our troops in Belgium, you know, and I did manage to find Germany."

Melanie laughed. Gem put her arms around the General, coming up to just above his knees. Melanie started to pull her away, but she clung to him.

"Please, come in," Melanie said. 'How *did* you find us?"

"Well, I think I scared the bejesus—sorry, sweetheart, I'm not used to being around little ones—out of your mother-in-law. It was just about six thirty when I knocked on her door. She shushed me, afraid I was going to awaken her guest."

"A boarder," Melanie said. "Come in. I'll make coffee. I did remember to pick up coffee at the market, but I'm afraid it's instant."

"Did you also remember tea?"

"I did, yes."

"Then, I'll have tea. And, I brought some donuts to celebrate the new house. I stopped in town at the bakery when I heard that you moved."

"I'm surprised that Abbey told you where we were."

"I think she was anxious to get me out of there before I woke up the neighborhood. Afraid I never did learn to whisper. They wouldn't let me near the front lines."

Melanie put on the kettle she picked up at the estate

sale and set the table with the few dishes she'd purchased.

The General took off his hat when he entered the house and looked around for some place to put his jacket.

"We don't have much furniture," Melanie said. "Let me hang those in the closet."

"Well," he said to Gem, taking her hand, "show me your new house. I'm anxious to see it." And show him she did. First, the back yard. She dragged the General from the bear's house to the tree and the cellar door and the spot in the back that was now grass but would one day be her garden. The General didn't quite get what she was trying to tell him about the grass area, but he pretended to.

Then inside. Her room with the bed and the dresser. Then her mother's room with bed, dresser and rug. The bathroom upstairs, then downstairs again to the empty living room and dining room and back to the kitchen.

"Very nice," General O'Brien said when he arrived back in the kitchen.

"I wish I could offer you some place to sit down," Melanie said, but we're rather shy of chairs at the moment."

"The back stoop will do just fine," General O'Brien said. "It's a lovely morning to eat outdoors."

And so they had their tea and hot chocolate on the back steps. Melanie and General O'Brien watched as Gem ran around the yard inspecting everything, every bush, every blossom, every branch.

"She'll be climbing that before long," the General remarked, nodding toward the big tree.

"I'm afraid so."

"What will you do with her when you go to work?"

Until then, Melanie realized that she hadn't told the General on the one occasion that they met about her drawings. "Let me show you," she said.

She went back inside and brought out her sketchpad. "I used to work at the airplane factory, "she said. She told him about the nose art with which he was familiar and fascinated.

"Tell me about that," he said.

"In a bit. Anyway," she went on, "two of my friends at the factory suggested, I think in jest, but I picked up on it, that I draw a comic strip. And here it is, *Warrior Woman.*"

The General took the sketchpad and studied it. "You drew this?"

Melanie nodded. "It appears in the Hearst papers, including ours here in town."

"I've seen it. Wonderful! How clever of you."

"And... the best part... I can work from home. The

editor in town sends a courier over every morning for my latest strip and then he forwards it to New York. I could take it to the post office myself, I guess, but I think he prefers that it comes from him. He has a kind of proprietorship about it."

"I don't blame him at all. He probably has some rights as well."Melanie hadn't thought about that, but she realized that it was no doubt true. Well, Mr. Meyers was the one to submit it to the Hearst publishers and he deserved compensation as well. Melanie did not begrudge him in the least, but she did wonder if Mr. Meyers had a share in the five year contract that she recently signed, perhaps in the small print. She would remember to ask the attorney the next time they met, if he wouldn't charge her for the information. Probably, he would.

"And with your new job, you purchased this house," the General was saying.

"Yes. I received a signing bonus which went for the down payment. And a five year contract which will cover the mortgage and allow us to live in a comfortable, not grand, but comfortable manner. We'll gradually fill the house with furnishings."

"I have a boatload full of furniture," the General said. "In my garage. From the house I closed in

Washington. Why don't I load it up this afternoon and have it delivered here?"

"Oh," was all that Melanie could say. She knew she should decline his generous offer, but she was so taken back by it, she just said again, "Oh."

Gem was clapping her hands. Until then, they didn't know that she was even listening, but she came over, climbed onto the General's lap, put her arms around his neck and kissed him on the cheek.

"Gem!"

"I think a kiss is more than ample payment. You may not want my old stuff, but it's certainly better than nothing at all. And the next time I come over, we'll have some place to sit, won't we, Princess?"

Without a second thought about it—because if she had given it a second thought she might not have done it— Melanie kissed the General's other cheek.

"Well, now, that is worth taking the two of you out to a big breakfast."

At four o'clock that afternoon, a truck pulled up in front of the little house on Oak Street. Two men got out and started carting in tables and chairs and a sofa and lamps (Melanie had forgotten about lamps until they went to turn on some lights the evening before and there were none), a round wooden table and four chairs which fit perfectly in the kitchen, rugs and drapes that could be hung until Melanie got around to hemming them, and silverware (it looked like real silver) and dishes and... it went on and on. The movers took over two hours to unload everything. When they were finished, Melanie went to get her purse to give them a tip, but the men refused it saying the General had taken care of it.

Gem was beside herself. She sat in every chair and the sofa, turned on every light, even swept the rugs with her bear's house broom, ran around touching everything.

At six o'clock, the General arrived in their driveway to see if everything was in order. He invited himself for dinner, which he brought with him. Margaret had been busy in their kitchen making stew and mashed potatoes and carrots and chocolate cake for the housewarming. Gem's eyes nearly popped when she saw the cake.

Melanie set the table which she had just given a good coat of polish. She found a tablecloth in a box that arrived in the kitchen marked, "linens". When the table was set, the kitchen filled with the aroma of food and polish and the scent of lilac from the back yard, Melanie invited the General and Gem to come inside for dinner. It couldn't be more perfect, Melanie thought, only if Edward were there to enjoy it with them. She said Grace: thanking God, thanking the General, and praying that one day soon Edward would be home to see their new home. "God bless General O'Brien," Melanie added before the blessing. Gem's head was bowed, hands together, eyes closed.

"Never felt so blessed," the General said.

On Sunday afternoon after church (they took the bus), Fred and Abigail came by with a plate of cookies. Melanie saw them arrive from the upstairs window. She watched as Abbey got out of the car, her mouth open, almost dropping the cookies in the street. Melanie called to Gem in the back yard and hurried to the front door to let them in.

"Welcome," Melanie said cheerfully.

Abigail's eyes took in everything. They moved from side to side, up and down and around, into this room and that room. "Where did you get this furniture?" she demanded. Definitely demanded.

"Most of it from General O'Brien."

Abigail snapped her head around. "What?"

"General O'Brien came by yesterday. He said he called at your house…"

"At six thirty in the morning on a Saturday. I would have choked him if he awakened my boarder…"

My boarder, Melanie said to herself.

Fred commented that, "The place looks great." Beside him, Abigail stiffened.

"How much did you have to pay him for all this?"

Melanie anticipated the question and was ready with an answer. "He's lending it to us until he puts it in storage or sells it or whatever he decides to do with it. But, it's certainly wonderful for us to have now, until we can afford some things of our own."

Abigail didn't comment on any of it specifically, but Melanie saw her giving the once over to the sofa and the upholstered armchairs in the living room and the drapes. The dining room was empty but the kitchen was well furnished. Abigail, however, refused to sit down. She placed the cookies on the polished table, running her finger over the surface.

Gem came running in the door, grabbed her grandpa's hand and dragged him outside.

"She doesn't even say hello," Abigail said.

"Forgive her, Abbey. She's so excited about the yard."

Abigail stiffened and lifted her head, her nostrils pinched like she smelled something rotten. "We have to get back," she said suddenly. "I have a roast in the oven."

"Some day soon, I'll have you and Fred over for dinner," Melanie said.

"Don't bother. I have a guest to feed each night. And we may be getting another boarder tomorrow. The college has called and asked if we could take in another one of their professors."

"Your table will be full, Abigail," Melanie said. She delighted in saying it. Originally, Abigail had not planned to spend all of her time in the kitchen, but it seemed to be working out that way. *What was it she said,* Melanie thought back. "Worn out from all those mouths to feed." (Fred, Melanie and little Gem, who ate practically nothing). Now, there may be two more grown appetites to feed. "Worn out" would not begin to cover the laundry, the cooking, the shopping, the cleanup and the invasion of their privacy, which Abigail so coveted.

Melanie wouldn't gloat. She wouldn't rejoice in it. Blessed are they who enjoy the good fortune of others. Wasn't that a beatitude? It should be, Melanie decided.

Muffin made an appearance *after* Abigail left. Gem took her upstairs to her room.

Chapter Fifteen

On Monday, after the bus picked up Gem for school, Melanie straightened the house before starting to work. The sun porch was cold early in the morning. She'd have to get some sort of space heater, she thought, if she were going to get any work done before noon, her best time for energy, inspiration, and quiet.

She was barely through with a load of laundry when the doorbell rang. So few people knew where she lived, she wondered... Through the stained glass window, she saw two men, one she definitely recognized.

"Hello," she said to General O'Brien. "You're up early this morning."

"Make hay while the sun shines or some rot," the big man said. "This is José, my handyman." Melanie nodded toward José whose hands were full of tools, measuring tape, leveler, plane, sundry screwdrivers, pliers, hammers hanging from his belt.

"He's going to make that sun porch of yours livable."

"Pardon?"

"You'll catch your death working out there this winter, even now I suspect."

"You're a mind-reader. I was just thinking about a space heater."

"Rubbish. Too dangerous for the child. Back here, José." And he proceeded to lead José to the back of the house.

"But...?" Melanie started, closing the door behind them.

"I'll have some of that coffee you make," the General said after he got José to measuring and told him what he thought should be done. "Don't mind, do you, that I've barged in here?"

"Of course, not. You can barge in here any time you like. It is cold, isn't it? Why don't we go into the kitchen."

Once settled in the kitchen, the General explained.

"I got to thinking last night about you trying to work in that room. That is where you plan to draw?"

"Yes. I guess I didn't really think too much about how chilly it would be in the morning."

"A lot to consider moving into a new house. I'm just getting a handle on that monster across the lake I bought. Good move though."

"Of course, it is. And for us, having you here in our community. You are such a… presence."

"A presence. I like that. I've been called lots of things, but I rather like being a 'presence.' Now, down to something I wanted to tell you yesterday, but I didn't want to speak in front of your little girl. She's a sharp one. I've noticed that when you think she's preoccupied, she's still listening with a very sharp ear to what's being said."

"You noticed, did you?"

"A very commendable trait in a child, curiosity and…"

"Snooping?"

"Yes, to put a blunt edge on it. Never hurts to be informed. Something else I've been wondering. You've investigated signing, I suppose."

Melanie nodded. "We have, but the counselors at school told me that if we start, Gem will substitute that for actually speaking. As far as any of the doctors have determined, there is nothing preventing her from speaking again. If we teach her to sign, she may never feel she needs language again."

The General frowned but after a thoughtful silence, he nodded, recognizing the logic in that decision. "I see," he said. "I've been working on locating your husband; I want you to know. It's a nightmare trying to get information out of the Germans." He leaned in to say confidentially, "I wouldn't want you to repeat this to anyone, but the good news is that the war in Europe is coming to an end, very soon. Days, not weeks."

Melanie squealed with delight.

"The bad news is that it may be months before we reinstate the prisoners of war. Some will never be found." He let that ominous news settle like a dark cloud over the sunny kitchen.

"Are you suggesting that we prepare ourselves for the worst?"

"Absolutely not. I never prepare for the worst. I always assume the outcome will be in our favor and work from strength, not from weakness or defeat. There is a very good chance that Corporal Commons was never a prisoner of war. I have learned through Army records and friends

I've prevailed upon, that your husband's unit was behind enemy lines when it was heard from last. In France."

"France?"

"Yes. I don't know if you've heard about the number of French people who have courageously hidden American soldiers from the Germans, at great risk of death by a firing squad for themselves and their families. Hundreds of our men have been rescued by the French underground."

"There's a chance…?"

"More than a chance. First, the camps. We'll be checking all of the camps for your corporal. When the armistice is signed, I expect within days, the French, Belgians, Italians, Swiss, all allies, including those under German rule, will give up their American servicemen to freedom. They are the real heroes of this war, the underground."

Melanie was overcome, tears pouring down her cheeks. She doubted that the General could abide such a display of emotion, but he reached in and handed her a perfectly folded, ironed handkerchief. She wiped her eyes. "I'll launder this," she said, but he took it back from her.

"It's sacred," he responded.

José had finished his measurements. He and the General had some words, in Spanish. In halting, broken

English, José asked Melanie if it would be convenient for him to come back later to begin construction. Melanie had no idea what he planned to do, but she was too emotional at the time to inquire. She nodded, smiled and put out her hand to José. The General nodded to her as well and they left.

The sun was bright, the kitchen bathed in its light as Melanie sat at the table, picked up her sketchpad and started drawing what was in her heart. It came rapidly, a sketch which she completed in a matter of two hours. After determining that it captured the "essence" of what she was feeling that morning, the tear-stained young wife picked up the phone to call Mr. Meyers.

Chapter Sixteen

Melanie's submission was picked up by courier on May 6th, 1945, two days before the armistice in Europe was announced. The comics the next day in the local paper as well as a banner across the front page below the masthead was Melanie's drawing in black and white of Warrior Woman with her arms around three servicemen.

The phone rang constantly that morning. A large bouquet of flowers arrived at the little house on Oak Street from the General. The card read, "How perceptive of you" as if he had nothing to do with the timing.

Tony and Marty called with shouts of congratulations each trying to drown out the other over the phone. Melanie said she would have them over to dinner very soon to celebrate. Fred came over to dance a jig with Melanie, his favorite way to celebrate. Nothing from Abigail, but Melanie had not expected it. It just didn't matter anymore. All Gem knew was that her mother had drawn something that was in the paper on the front page. As far as she was concerned, it was a picture of her daddy on the left and she took it to her room.

Was the house ready for guests? Ready or not, Melanie dug out her recipe file. Just as she was making a grocery list, there was an unexpected call from Mary Jo. First, the congratulations. "Everybody in town is talking about you." And then the real reasons for her call, first and second. "I'm dying to see all this wonderful furniture the General gave you."

Gossips! "Not 'gave me,'" Melanie said, perhaps too quickly, "loaned me until he decides if he wants to store it or sell it or just what he plans to do with it."

"Well, I'm just dying to see it. I'd also love to meet him. One of his assistants had picked out the house for him, so I never got to meet him personally."

Could she be any more obvious? Wondering later why in the world she did it, in a weak moment Melanie invited Mary Jo to dinner with a couple of friends to celebrate the banner.

All giggly, Mary Jo practically jumped through the phone. "Will *he* be there?" she asked.

"The General?" *What had she done?* "I haven't asked," she said.

"Will you? I am just…"

"I know, dying to meet him. Well, we can't have the only real estate agent in town dying, can we?" It was a slur, but she didn't seem to get it.

"What can I bring? I make a wonderful tart."

Melanie held her tongue. "Fine," she said, setting aside the dessert file. "Bring your… tart."

Water off a duck's back. She didn't get it.

So, the party was set for Friday evening. Marty and Tony accepted almost as enthusiastically as Mary Jo, but with no giggles. "Informal," Melanie told them, realizing that she'd forgotten to tell Mary Jo that, but didn't want to call her back.

Fortunately, the General was available and would bring wine. "Red or white?" he asked.

"Whatever you think," Melanie said.

"What's the entrée?"

"Oh." She quickly grabbed her file, saw the first recipe on top, chicken casserole. "Chicken," she said. It looked fairly simple.

"Good. White then. What time?"

"How's seven?" Melanie laughed. "At Abigail's, we'd be finished with dinner and ready for bed at seven."

The General laughed. "Not too late for Gem, is it, to stay up?"

"No," Melanie said. "It isn't a school night."

"Perfect. I'd like to have her with us at dinner."

What a refreshing change, actually wanting Gem to participate in adult time. Melanie so wished she could invite Fred, but there was no way he'd be allowed to come alone. And she would not include Abigail and her boarders. Some time soon, she knew she'd have to make an appearance and introduce herself to the boarders, but not this time. This was her evening.

It was turning into quite an event. Melanie spent a tidy sum—an amount she would have given to Abigail a month before to help defray the cost of groceries—on candles and flowers and colorful throw pillows everywhere. She even had time to construct, although she hid the unprofessional seams, a pad that fit the ledge of the fireplace shelf for extra seating. It was a bright orange, picking up a color in the chintz upholstery and brightening the room considerably.

The sun porch was under construction. José was coming on the following Monday when the materials he needed would be available. That left the living room for sitting before the meal. Once Mary Jo invited herself *and* the General, Melanie realized with a start that there was no room to dine except the kitchen. She couldn't call the General and ask if he by any chance had a dining room table and six chairs in his attic that he wasn't using. So, after Gem was picked up for school, she took the bus downtown to the second hand store.

There was a table. It needed refinishing, but with a cloth over it, no one would know. It was reasonable, actually of oak, and would fit beautifully into the house-of-mixed-woods, as it might be so aptly named. There were four chairs that kind of matched and two that didn't, but some day, Melanie thought, she would have them stripped and stained to match the table. For now, however, it was what she could afford. If she took the chairs, the proprietor agreed to deliver everything at no charge.

"Today?" Melanie asked.

Earlier, when she walked into the store, the owner recognized her immediately and proudly showed her his copy of the paper with her banner on top. He agreed to deliver the dining room set that day. Melanie doubted she would have gotten such accommodation if the owner had customers lined up behind her or if he wasn't curious, like everyone else in town that Mary Jo talked to, about the little house that the comic strip artist bought. Maybe what the owner wanted to see was the house-that-the-General furnished with antiques.

Later that afternoon when his truck arrived in the driveway with a helper, the shop owner himself came in to see where the furniture should go, taking his time to look around. "You ever decide to upgrade this junk," he said, debasing the furniture, "let me know. Tourists go for this early twentieth century look."

Melanie had no doubt that the General's "early-twentieth-century look" would be listed as "estate antiques" if the second hand store ever got their hands on it.

"My stuff's better quality," he said admiring the dining room once the table and chairs were in place. "You want an heirloom lace tablecloth? I can drop one off on my way home tonight."

No, Melanie did not want or need an heirloom lace tablecloth and she certainly didn't want the little banty rooster, roving-eyed shop owner stopping by on his way home that night, or ever. "I have one," she said, fully aware that he didn't believe her, but who cared anyway.

After a polish, the dining room set looked halfway decent. With a cloth over the table, it looked more than halfway decent and with dimmed lights, candles and flowers and the General's silverware, it looked magnificent.

Marty and Tony arrived first. They brought wine. Melanie didn't know anything about wine, but when the General arrived later with three bottles of wine with corks, not screw tops, she felt badly for Marty and Tony. But, they didn't seem to mind in the least. They were too in awe of the General's presence, accepting with pleasure the glass of wine that he poured them. Immediately, Tony and Marty jumped in and asked questions about the General's role in the war.

Gem, with her fruit juice, sat on the now-covered shelf in front of the fireplace and listened. She seemed very grown up to Melanie in her little pinafore and sandals, sitting there attentively, not pestering anyone, seemingly happy to be included in the adult talk. Abigail always asked if it wasn't "the child's" bedtime whenever she, Fred and Melanie went into the parlor to talk. However, the talk was usually unpleasant and Gem was always happy to go to her room.

Mary Jo made her appearance at seven o'clock, the hour that Melanie planned to serve the casserole. She arrived ("festooned" is the only word Melanie could think of) in some elaborate costume complete with feathers, four inch high heels and her homemade dessert.

"I made this especially for you," she told the General holding the dish up to his nose after she'd been introduced to everyone. "It's a tart."

Melanie didn't dare look at either Marty or Tony and it appeared that the General, also, was having trouble keeping a smile from escaping. Mary Jo sat on the sofa next to the General, her legs crossed, her short skirt inching up her thighs.

"Please excuse us," Melanie said, once everyone was settled. "Gem, will you help me in the kitchen."

Gem was only too happy to get away from Mary Jo. Melanie knew that look and the way her daughter avoided sitting or standing anywhere near the woman who was wearing bird feathers around her neck. When Mary Jo talked—and talked she did the entire evening—she dangled the boa of feathers with her left hand. The General turned aside once, Melanie noticed, to pluck a feather out of his wine.

Gem served the salads after Melanie showed her on which side of the plate to place them. It hadn't occurred to Melanie that the only good glasses she had were being used in the living room for wine. There was nothing to do when she invited everyone to come and sit down but to ask them if they would bring their wine glass with them.

Once they were seated, the General across from Mary Jo, Gem at one head of the table, Marty and Tony across from each other, Melanie served the casserole on the dinner plates the General had given her, and sat down at the other head of the table—the one closest to the kitchen—to join them.

"Will you say Grace, General?"

The General recited a beautiful poem that his grandmother had taught him as a child whenever the family gathered. Melanie asked if he would write it down for her. Mary Jo went on about her family's traditions in the south until finally Marty broke in on her with, "This is wonderful," referring to the dinner.

"Excellent," General O'Brien agreed. "My grandmother's plates never served anything so delicious."

"Aren't you just a savior," Mary Jo said, "coming to this poor young wife's rescue with furniture and china and…" she held up a knife… "silver."

"Beautiful things are meant to be enjoyed," he said, and for some reason he flushed. Melanie saw Marty glance at Tony across the table, but not at her, then looked quickly away.

The meal turned out great, but the undertow disturbed Melanie profoundly. What were Mary Jo, Marty and Tony thinking? She had a husband. The white haired man at the table, who had lavished gifts on her, was old enough to be her grandfather. Just let them say one word to me, Melanie thought, and I'll set them straight fast.

The subject turned to Melanie's comics and the banner in the local paper. Mary Jo remained quiet, trying to interrupt several times with questions for the General about his war experiences or gossip about people in town, but Marty and Tony seemed hell-bent on not letting her into the table talk any more. They told the General about Melanie's nose art, her days at the factory in great detail, making Melanie blush. She tried to change the subject several tines, but either Tony or Marty would come up with some new story about the factory, some which Melanie never heard before.

"And, so what's Warrior Woman up to these days?" Marty asked, "now that we're not at war."

"Not at war?" the General boomed. "What do you call that massacre in the Pacific?"

Marty went all red and apologized. "Sorry, General," he said, "I should have said at war with

Germany."

"War won't be over until…" The General stopped. Everyone at the table was aware that he was about to say something that probably he shouldn't, perhaps the wine loosening his tongue, but he recovered in time to add, "until all our young men and women are back home. Which, reminds me, Mrs. Commons…" (Melanie didn't miss the 'Mrs. Commons'), "you have neglected women in service in your art."

"You're absolutely right, General," Melanie said. To everyone present that evening, they were Mrs. Commons and the General. "I'll take care of that in my next drawing."

"Good girl."

And so the meal went. Not too uncomfortable. Not uncomfortable at all by the time Mary Jo served the tart and the General poured more wine.

Gem went upstairs about nine o'clock after kissing everyone goodnight. The General hugged her for several seconds, thanked her for being such a charming hostess and helper, and kissed her on the forehead. You couldn't miss his devotion to her. The guests certainly picked up on it: Marty and Tony with big smiles, Mary Jo watching, but not smiling.

After Melanie insisted that no one could help her

clear the table or clean up the kitchen, and Mary Jo insisted that the General take the rest of the tart home with him (that being the hardest comment of all to hear without smiling), Marty and Tony kissed Melanie goodnight. They both worked hard to avoid looking at Melanie or each other and risk the grin.

The General bucked at Mary Jo's remark trying to hang back and not leave with her, but she said, "May I lean on you, General? These heels just seem to find every single crack in that sidewalk."

And then they were gone. Melanie cleared the table, made a soapy sink with warm water and hand washed each plate carefully. While washing and drying every single piece of china and the dime store glasses, she had time to think. Thinking back to Mary Jo's comments made her shake her head and smile. Marty and Tony's quick looks made her cringe. And General O'Brien calling her Mrs. Commons all night made her thoughtful.

After she turned out the lights later and went upstairs to her room, checking to be sure that Gem was asleep, Melanie wondered what Mary Jo would have to say to anyone who pumped her for details.

She wouldn't have to wait long. The next morning Gem was outside pulling weeds with her little hoe and spade in the garden that she and Fred had planted when the doorbell rang. Melanie saw who it was before she opened the door. "You're up early," she said.

Mary Jo was wearing sunglasses and a stole around her bare arms. "May I come in?"

"Of course. Would you like some coffee?"

"I'd kill for it."

"Well, don't kill anything." Melanie could tell from Mary Joe's demeanor that she was upset. The thought ran through her mind, *the General didn't- He didn't- Or, maybe he hadn't and that's what was upsetting her.*

"I made a fool of myself, didn't I?"

Melanie was so taken back that she didn't immediately respond, which sounded for all the world like she agreed. "What?" she said, recovering. "I don't know what you mean."

"Oh, be honest. I threw myself at him, didn't I?"

"The General?"

"Well, of course, the General. Who else? Not those blue collar friends of yours."

That did not sit well. "Mary Jo..." Melanie started to say-

"Sorry," she said. Then, she started to cry. "I'm so disappointed. I wanted him to be dazzled. I overdid it,

167

didn't I? I haven't been eating—dieting—and I guess that wine went right to my head. And my mouth."

"Mary Jo, you're too hard on yourself."

"Don't patronize me, Mel."

Mel? No one but Edward ever called her Mel.

"I just want another chance. Do you think it would be out of line if I went over to his house and apologized?"

"I don't think it would be out of line, but I think it isn't necessary."

"Oh, but it is, and I want to see him again. I know he'll never call me after last night. All that macho army crap. He's scared of women."

"Scared?"

"Of course, scared. You have to cozy up to a man like that slowly, not like a runaway train coming at him. I should have been helpless, like you."

Melanie was too shocked to say anything.

"Will you help me?"

"Do what?"

"Call on him with me. Let's bring him some cookies or something."

"Mary Jo, the General has a wonderful housekeeper who can bake rings around either one of us. I don't think she'd appreciate us showing up with a plate of cookies."

"Well, what can I do?" She was frantic, tears streaming down her face.

Melanie glanced out the window and noticed that Gem was still busy with her garden.

"I may have an idea." Something did just occur to Melanie. "Do you know Mr. Meyers at the paper?"

"Why? What have you heard?"

"Heard? Nothing. I just asked if you knew him."

"Of course, I know him. Better than I care to admit."

Oh!

"Well, what if you talked Mr. Meyers into a house and garden preview of how the Walker house has been converted into the General's home. You could bring Mr. Meyers with you to talk to the General."

Mary Jo was staring at Melanie, no expression on her face that Melanie could read.

"How did you think of that?"

Melanie shrugged. Before she could admit that it just sprang into her head, Mary Jo jumped up and headed for the front door. "Genius," she said. "I have to get my hair done."

"Mary Jo," Melanie called. "Don't over do it."

The already scheming woman turned around,

smiled, and nodded. "Thank you," she said. Melanie thought it was the first sincere thing out of her mouth yet.

Chapter Seventeen

José arrived early Monday morning, so early, in fact, that Melanie was frightened when she heard the knock at the door, thinking someone had died. Instead, she was greeted by José's smiling face.

"Buenos días, señora."

"Good morning, José. You're early."

"Disculpame, eh, I am sorry. I bring donuts, from the, eh, bakery."

"Oh, how sweet of you. Come in, I'll get some coffee brewing and we can enjoy them."

While Melanie prepared the coffee, José set up his work area. The sun peeked through; the dusty blues and deep purples of dawn illuminated the backyard. By the time José was set up, the sun through the trees dispersed the light into wispy strands along the walls and ceiling. Melanie brought out a plate with three donuts and a cup of coffee. José thanked her and set the food beside his ladder. He sipped the coffee, watching the sun ascend toward the tree tops, as Gem came down the stairs. She watched José admiring the scenery and smiled. He glanced at her and raised his cup, nodding kindly. She nodded back and then charged into the kitchen.

Once José started working, he did not notice Gem setting out her toys nearby. She was ready for school later that morning and was biding her time before the special bus arrived. José did not pay attention to her until a butterfly landed on the window sill and noticed that Gem stopped playing with her bears. She got up, walked over to the butterfly, extended her hand, and the creature hopped into her palm. Its wings were red and gold, with black spots along the edges. Gem caressed the wings. The butterfly didn't move. José watched in awe as the child touched the creature with her nose. The butterfly slowly flapped its wings, as though in greeting. Then, it turned and flew away.

"Mariposa," he said, and she smiled, touching her hands over her heart.

And from that moment on, whenever José was in the house, Gem would only respond to the name "Mariposa". Melanie came to prefer the word over the English butterfly, and found herself calling Gem by the name even when José wasn't around.

The butterfly returned every morning while José worked, and one day he decided to approach it. He walked tentatively, expecting it to flutter off, but it stayed. He held out his fist, extending each finger one by one, until his palm lay out directly under the creature. It flapped its wings slowly, as it had with Gem, and then hopped onto his palm. He marveled at the creature, so content, flapping its wings slowly, the early morning sun kissing the edges of its wings. Another hand came out, and the butterfly leapt to it. Out of the corner of his eye, he saw Gem, who must have seen the whole thing. She met his stare and her eyes scrunched up with joy. He had never heard her make a sound, but he could have sworn at that moment to have heard the slightest squeal.

Later that same day, José made his finishing touches and said good bye. Melanie insisted he come over for dinner one night. When Gem threw her arms around his neck, José thought for sure that he heard a "thank you" whispered in his ear. He pulled back and Gem smiled at him.

"¿Puedes hablar?"

The girl smiled, giving him a knowing look.

"What's that?" Melanie asked.

José was about to translate what he had said, that Gem had talked, when he noticed the alarm that crept into her face.

"Nothing," he said. "I will miss my Mariposa is all."

"You're welcome here anytime, José."

"Gracias, señora, thank you."

The girls watched his truck disappear in the distance. Melanie looked at Gem, who appeared distraught.

"Is something wrong, honey?"

Without looking at her mother, she turned around and walked back inside. The butterfly didn't return to the sill the next day, or the day after.

Chapter Eighteen

On one of his weekly visits to see how things were going and to check on Gem, Fred hung around the sun porch more than usual. He definitely seemed to have something on his mind. "What is it, Fred?" Melanie asked after awhile. Gem was busy outside pulling weeds.

"I think you should stop by to meet the new boarder," he said.

"All right," Melanie said. "When would be a good time?"

"He's usually at the house on Sundays."

"And what time? I don't want to come at meal time unannounced."

"Oh, sure. Sure. So, after church then, two o'clock? Abbey's usually paring vegetables Sunday afternoons." Fred paused to look out at Gem's garden. "I think those carrots will be ready by Sunday."

It was not an occasion Melanie looked forward to, but she told Gem that it would be a very thoughtful thing to do, after church, to bring her grandmother some home grown vegetables. Gem didn't seem thrilled at the idea, but early Sunday morning, before she got dressed, she went out into her garden and picked some carrots. Three.

"Maybe more," Melanie said when she saw how few Gem was willing to part with, "...and maybe some radishes and lettuce. Grand Abbey has a boarder to feed now."

Dutifully, Gem picked a basket of vegetables, came in, hopped up on the chair which she dragged over to the sink, and washed them carefully, the way her mother taught her. They were a fine looking bunch of home grown vegetables, Melanie said. She wrapped them in clean white paper and put them in the refrigerator until later.

As fortune or misfortune would have it, Melanie and Gem sat in a pew opposite Abigail and Fred in church that morning. Gem waved to them and Melanie was pleased to see that Abigail nodded to her. As they were walking out, unavoidably in proximity to each other, Melanie said, "We'd like to stop by later, if that's all right. Gem has some homegrown vegetables which she picked this morning for you."

Abigail looked down at Gem and actually smiled. "We finish lunch about twelve thirty," she said. "Any time after that would be fine."

"All right then," Melanie said, aware that they had not been invited to lunch. No matter. Actually, better. "Two o'clock," Melanie said and turned to speak to the Pastor.

Gem ran once they reached Abbey and Fred's street at exactly two o'clock that afternoon. She raced ahead to the house while Melanie watched from behind. Gem entered the house without knocking, like she always did but that was close on to two months ago now and a lot had changed since then.

When Melanie came to the open door, Abigail was standing there with a tall, very thin man in his fifties, Melanie judged. He had gray hair and a matching, almost sickly looking complexion. Melanie hoped her initial reaction to the boarder didn't show.

"The child's forgotten her manners," were the first words out of Abigail's mouth.

"I think she still thinks of this as home," Melanie

said in defense of her daughter. She stuck out her hand, "I'm Melanie Commons, Edward's wife."

"How very nice to meet you," the man said, "I'm Professor Pointer." He seemed very pleasant.

Abigail had set out a plate of cookies in the den.

There was lemonade on a tray, and Abigail's homemade oatmeal cookies which Gem hated. She had heard her grandmother say constantly, "They're good for you," which is probably why Gem took a huge dislike to them. She much preferred her mother's butter cookies, like her daddy used to make at the bakery for her. The funny thing, Abigail knew that Gem hated oatmeal cookies. *Then who were they for, or why be so obvious?* Maybe Abigail was happier with Gem outside.

"What do you teach at the college, Professor?" Melanie asked once they were seated. Abigail asked Melanie to pour, which she did, and passed the cookies.

"Political science," Professor Pointer said.

Melanie knew nothing about politics, had no idea what to say beyond, "How interesting."

"I'm very sorry about your husband," Professor Poitnter said. "Such a waste of our young men."

"Waste?" Melanie said. She couldn't let that go by with no response.

"Not our war," the Professor said glibly. "Roosevelt's in bed with that warmonger, Churchill."

Melanie was about to explode. Abigail must have sensed it. "Professor Pointer has a magnificent collection of operas on LP's," she said quickly. "We listen to opera every night."

"How... enjoyable for you," Melanie said politely. She wanted to add, *"And for Fred."* No wonder Fred stopped by to see Gem several evenings a week.

"Do you like opera?" Professor Pointer asked Melanie.

There was no getting around it. If she said "yes", he'd probably suggest that they listen to one. "I'm sorry, no," she said bravely, not looking at Abigail. "I haven't really become acquainted with opera. I hear an aria now and then on the radio that I like, but I couldn't tell you what it is or who the composer was, I'm afraid." She cleared her throat, took a drink of her lemonade. "Have you seen the deer?" she asked, obviously changing the subject.

"No," Abigail said firmly.

"Deer?" Professor Pointer asked.

"A small deer that used to visit when Gem played in the back yard," Melanie said.

"The child has fantasies," as Abigail explained it. "I

understand you had a dinner party recently." Another abrupt change of subject.

"Yes," Melanie admitted. "Several people who had been very kind to me in the move."

"I was thrilled to know that it was Abbey's daughter-in-law who'd drawn that picture on the front page of the paper," Professor Pointer said. "Comics are such an amusement for the proletariat."

Melanie felt as though she had just been slapped. Too stunned to say anything, she tried to follow along with Abbey who turned the subject to the Professor Pointer's hobby of mounting and researching various species of butterflies. *Fascinating.* For twenty minutes Melanie tried to keep an enraptured look on her face as Professor Pointer educated her on the various butterflies in the area vis-a-vis (his words) those in other parts of the world.

At one point Fred started to come into the room, became aware of the topic of conversation, and quickly slipped back out with Gem. Nothing in there for them, dead butterflies and oatmeal cookies.

No inquiries from Abigail about her granddaughter's school progress or Melanie's art on behalf of the "proletariat." So, after all that she could take and then some, Melanie stood up to leave. She certainly didn't want professor Pointer to bring out his butterfly collection pinned to a board. She would have gotten Gem and bolted out of there before she'd let that happen.

"It's been very interesting *listening* to you," Melanie said, wondering if they would get her emphasis on her exaggerated use of the word. "But we need to take some flowers to a neighbor who is ill."

"Just like your mother-in-law," Professor Pointer said. "All this devotion to others. So commendable."

Yes, we love the proletariat, Melanie wished she had the nerve to say. She retrieved Gem from the garden, glanced at Fred who looked away from her, and took their leave. She'd been wrong. It wasn't Abigail who wanted her to visit. It was Fred. He *wanted* Melanie to meet the boarder. *Why? Perhaps Fred wanted Melanie to know how he was suffering. Opera. Butterflies. Politics. The insufferable proletariat.*

Gem skipped home, carefully avoiding the cracks in the sidewalk playing, "Step on a Crack, Break Your Mother's Back", a game Melanie herself had played as a child.

Walking alone except at intersections where Gem waited for her mother to catch up and hold her hand while crossing the streets, Melanie thought about the professor. If

Abigail had hopes of replacing Edward in her life, she was welcome to the substitute. They were approaching the bus stop when a horn honked behind them. Fred.

He leaned out the window. "I'll drive you home," he said. *Now what?* They got in, Melanie in front, Gem in the back. "I forgot to give you these books," Fred said to Gem when they started for home. "I picked them up at the book store. All you could put in a paper sack for two dollars."

"How kind of you, Fred," Melanie said, though she didn't for a minute believe that was why he came after them to drive them home. He could have brought them to the house on one of his visits. Melanie decided to wait until Fred mentioned what it was that was upsetting him, because he did look shaken, Melanie would have said if anyone asked.

"What am I going to do about that bore?" He said it right out loud with Gem in the back seat looking at the books.

"Fred?"

"I don't care if she hears me. I'm going crazy. They listen to opera every night, all day Saturday and Sunday. He catches butterflies and..." He glanced into the rear view mirror. Melanie jabbed him with her elbow.

"And lets them go, right?" Melanie said.

"Yeah. Lets them go. Not like how they land on her hand." He nodded toward the back seat. "She kisses 'em. You ever see her do that?"

"Yes," Melanie said. "All the time. The General sent over his..." She hadn't planned to tell Fred about José working at the house and was sorry that she opened up the subject. She let it die in mid sentence. Fred, very irate with a "woman driver" trying to turn right from a left lane in front of him, was trying hard to keep his cool with Gem in the back seat. He let the subject die. He would find out the next time he came over, but Melanie hoped she could think of something by then. It was a job Fred never could have handled. If he had been the one to suggest it, it would have taken months to complete, if ever. But knowing that another handyman was helping his daughter-in-law and granddaughter would hurt him, Melanie was sure, and she wouldn't hurt Fred for the world. She'd think of something. Fortunately, Fred couldn't come in that afternoon. He was on his way to the market for some olives for the Professor's drink.

"Alcohol?" Melanie said, shocked.

"The one bright spot in my day. I join him with a bit of schnapps when he has his martini."

"Who goes into the state liquor store to purchase the

alcohol?"

"Who do you think? I manage to pick myself up a pint or two while I'm there. He winked. "Never thought I'd see the day when Abbey would have a drink."

"Abbey drinks?"

"Sherry. Just to keep the professor company while they listen to opera. I have mine in the garage while I'm working. Sometimes..." He winked and then corrected himself, "...most times, two."

Melanie laughed. "Well now, Fred, life isn't so bad for you, is it?"

"Not so long as I got my radio in the garage and my pint stashed in the paint can. But, I'd prefer it if I could sit in the kitchen and listen to my programs." They were sitting in the car in the driveway, talking. Melanie put her arms around Fred and hugged him. "Make a life for yourself, Fred," she said. "You've earned it."

He looked at her. "You're right, daughter," he said. "I earned it. Right after dinner tonight, I'm going in the kitchen and turn on the radio to my programs. Let him listen to that opry stuff upstairs if he wants to."

"You know what, Fred. I'll bet Abbey will join you. I'm sure by now she's had all the culture she can stand. As I recall, she loved listening to Major Bowes and the Shadow with you."

"You're right about that. I'm even going into the den with my radio and sit in my rocker. Thank you, daughter. You always know how to handle her."

"With kid gloves, Fred," Melanie said, smiling. "Be kind. I know how much she misses Edward. This boarder is just someone to distract her from her sadness." Melanie suddenly remembered that Gem was in the back seat. She was sitting with an open book in her lap, but she was looking out the window. When she looked at her mother, her eyes were filled with her own personal sadness.

Communion

Chapter Nineteen

Several weeks went by with no word from either the General or Fred other than Fred's visits when Gem was home from school. He mentioned that Abbey had taken to going with the Professor to the college for lectures. And he grinned. That was perfectly all right with Fred. Melanie figured that, left alone, Fred could do whatever he damned pleased in his own house. Sounded like a solution for both of them. No one was asking her advice, so Melanie decided that as long as they were both contented, that's really all she could hope would happen.

The article with pictures of what was now known as the General's house appeared in one of the Sunday editions of the local paper. Color pictures of the grounds were featured. Nothing of the inside was shown. Melanie could only imagine that was at the General's request. He would insist on a certain amount of privacy and security and none could blame him, but the grounds were impressive with the newly installed flower beds and patio. Melanie and Gem had not seen the patio when they were there. It may have been under construction at the time. There was no doubt from the pictures that "The General's Manor" was certainly one of the finest estates in all of Erieville and would forever be called just that. The article spoke to the community, saying that the Brigadier General had made his mark, layered his contribution onto the history of this small town and picturesque lake.

Melanie and Gem settled into a routine of school and work and not much else. It was a surprise, then, for Melanie when her doorbell rang one Friday morning while Gem was in school. Unaccustomed to callers, she was in paint splattered jeans and tee shirt, hair tied back off her neck in a clip.

"Hello, is the lady of the house in?" General O'Brien said when she opened the door.

"What...?"

"Oh, it is you. I thought you might be the baby

sitter. You look about twelve."

"Well, if I'd known you were coming, General, I would have at least put on makeup. Come in. How have you been?"

"Busy," he said, entering.

"Coffee? Tea?"

"I'm afraid I can't stay. I stopped by to tell you that I'm going abroad on special assignment."

"Please, sit down. Can you at least sit down?"

He came into the kitchen and sat at the table. "In response to my inquiry about the evacuated prisoner of war camps, I've been asked by the Army Chief of Staff to conduct an on-site inspection of the camps for the historical record."

Melanie dared not say what she hoped.

"Of course," the General said, "if in the course of my investigation I should run across any information on the whereabouts of one Corporal Edward Commons, well, that would be all for the good." He gave her just the barest hint of a smile. The old fox, Melanie thought. More likely it had been his suggestion to the Army Chief of Staff that he personally conduct such an investigation, God bless him.

"I don't know what to say except that I will be praying for the success of your mission."

"Excellent." He stood. "Much to do, I'm afraid. I have to prepare for the winter, just in case I don't return before the first frost. I'm looking for someone trustworthy to keep an eye on my place. What about that father-in-law of yours?"

"Fred? Oh, General, I would trust Fred with my life, or Gem's. And I have on many occasions."

"Have him stop by to see me, will you. It has to be today. I should be back home by five o'clock. I'll walk him through the turn-off valves, in case of a frozen pipe or some such rot."

"He's very conscientious, General."

"Good. I'll expect him then. Well, my dear, take care of yourself and your daughter while I'm gone. I hope to have good news for you upon my return."

"General... I know the news may not be good, but promise me that you'll let me know if you hear anything about Edward, anything at all. I'd rather hear it from you than from a courier arriving at my door some morning."

"I promise, my dear. Brave of you to want to know. By the way, I thoroughly enjoyed myself at your dinner party. That friend of yours, Mary Jo? She's a kick in the pants, isn't she? Good for a laugh or two."

"I'm sure she enjoyed your company as well."

"When I get back, maybe we'll invite her over for cocktails. Would that be all right, do you think?"

"Of course. She was very interested to meet you. I'm sure she was a bit nervous at the dinner party. I doubt that she is as talkative as she was that night."

"Oh, that's all right. I'm a bit of a stodgy fellow myself. Don't know what to say around women. But that's my secret, my dear. When I get back... we'll see."

Melanie saw him out. She watched him pull his big car out of the drive, nearly knocking over the mailbox as he backed out—a man used to a driver.

What a wonderful occupation for Fred. Just what he needed now. Melanie phoned him immediately.

Two days later while Melanie was in town ordering supplies for her drawings, she saw Mary Jo through the front window of the real estate office on the phone. Melanie did not plan to stop, but Mary Jo saw her and waved her in.

"I'll pick you up at eight this evening and we'll have a look-see," Mary Jo said to whomever she was talking to on the phone. "You're just going to love this house, sugar, but you better be prepared to move quickly. There are four other buyers about ready to make an offer." She hung up.

"Hi," Melanie said. "You are the busy one."

"That?" she said, nodding toward the phone. "A lookeeloo. The house is a dump, but it looks better at night. How are you?"

"Fine," Melanie said. "That was a wonderful article in the Home and Garden section on the General's house."

Mary Jo shrugged. "I'm still waiting for him to call me. I told him I had some investment property that he really should take a look at, but I haven't heard from him."

"You know that he left for Europe."

"What? No!"

"A special assignment. He stopped by to tell me. And he mentioned how much he enjoyed the dinner party. Asked about you."

"He did? Sit down. Tell me everything." Melanie did. There wasn't much to tell, but she could see that Mary Jo was hanging on every word.

"Oh, Sugar, that is just the best news ever. I would so love to be his wife."

Melanie gasped. "Mary Jo, I didn't mean to encourage you beyond-"

"I know, I know, I'm just glad he wasn't turned off by my chatter. I don't know when to stop when I'm nervous and I was so nervous that evening. I did so want to make a good impression. You will keep me posted, won't you, if you hear from him again, and tell him I'm looking forward to a quiet dinner party, just the two of us."

"I don't know that I will be hearing from him, but if I do, I'll certainly tell him." Melanie wasn't so sure that a "quiet dinner party" was something that the General had in mind, but that was for him to decide.

"Listen, Sugar, I want you to come to my party this weekend. Lots of wonderful, interesting people, different backgrounds. You'll fit right in and they will just love you."

"Mary Jo, I don't go to parties, not since…"

"I know, Sugar, but these are just some nice people in town that you should get to know. After all, Precious, you are a professional now and you need to mingle with people who can do you some good. You never know if who you're talking to could open doors you can't even imagine. I only have the brightest, up and coming zillionaires at my parties. Let me send someone to pick you up."

"No, no."

"Come on now, Sugar, you're way too young and pretty to be sitting at home Saturday nights. You come to my house and I'll take good care of you. You'll meet some fascinating people. I'll send a driver around eight. I won't take no for an answer now, you hear."

And before Melanie could decline gracefully, the

phone rang and Mary Jo was back in her agent mode.

I can always call and tell her I can't make it, Melanie said to herself as she walked back to the house.

Chapter Twenty

Every single day that week Melanie had the best of intentions of calling Mary Jo and making some excuse for not attending her party. She even dialed twice, but the line was busy. Then, it was Saturday morning. Fred stopped by and Melanie found herself asking if he would be available to come over and stay with Gem while she went to a meeting. It wasn't exactly a fib. She would be meeting new people. Fred was delighted to come by and stay with Gem. He would spend the night in the spare room so Melanie wouldn't worry about the time she returned home.

"What will Abbey say?" Melanie asked.

"She won't even know I'm not there," he said. "They

listen to the opera on the radio Saturday nights. I'm not allowed to run my band saw in the garage while it's on. I'll tell her that I'm fixing some cabinets at your house and plan to stay over and finish on Sunday."

So it was arranged. Melanie had that little black dress and her pearls, high heels, a black clutch bag she bought once at a yard sale and never used and a very pretty lime green shawl which Edward bought her one Christmas. Gem was looking forward to playing with Grandpa and having him spend the night. Melanie couldn't decline now. And besides, it was already Saturday.

Just in case Mary Jo told the driver to come up to get her, Melanie was outside waiting at eight o'clock when he arrived. And she didn't want him getting out of the car to open the door for her, especially when she saw a handsome, young man pull into the driveway. Melanie walked quickly around the car to the passenger side, held up her hand to wave and indicated to the driver that she could get the door herself. A quick wave fluttered out to Gem and Fred who might be watching from the front window finalized her departure, although Gem had dragged her Grandpa outside to the playhouse he was building for her and paid her no mind. To an empty entry hall, Melanie had called before leaving that she was going, she had her key, and not to wait up for her.

By the time Melanie and her driver arrived at Mary Jo's glass house on the hill, she knew three things about her escort. He was an agent friend of Mary Jo's, divorced, and new in town. Mary Jo had made him an offer to join her realty company, he said, and he was in the process of making the move from Atlanta. *The southern accent,* Melanie said to herself. Mary Jo was from Atlanta, where she and Ted—his name—grew up together.

"And what about you?" he asked as they were pulling in the driveway. "Mary Jo tells me that you're an artist."

"Yes," Melanie said. *How nice to be identified as an artist.*

"And your husband…?"

Good. He knew she had a husband.

"In the Army," Melanie said, not wishing to elaborate. A party was not the time to be talking about a husband *missing in action.*

The party was in full swing when they entered the large entry. The room to the right was a small ballroom in size, furnished with white sofas and white chairs and glass and wrought iron cocktail tables; flowers everywhere, peach and purple and white. Thank God she didn't clip some roses from the garden as she originally thought to do. The only thing that prevented her from making that horrible error was the fact that the roses were past their prime. As Melanie looked around the room at the smartly dressed young people, she wondered if that wasn't true about her as well.

She accepted a glass of something bubbly, non alcoholic the server said from a tray of mixed drinks. "Well, here she is," a slightly inebriated older man said loudly, "our resident cartoonist. Love that buxom woman you draw with the cute little ass."

If there had been a hole, Melanie would have stepped into it.

"Now don't you say anything lewd, Frank." It was John Meyers, the editor of the local paper and, technically, Melanie's boss. He redirected the weaving man, who insisted on putting his arm around Melanie, toward the dining room table. "Let's eat something, Frank," John Meyers suggested to Melanie's back.

"Sorry about that," Ted said. "There's one at every party, right?"

Melanie tried to smile. She sipped her drink and looked around for a friendly face. Outside of John Meyers, there didn't appear to be anyone she recognized in the room.

"Let's walk out on the patio," Ted suggested. "There's a lovely view of the countryside from up here."

The word still echoed in Melanie's ear. *Cartoonist.* It made her sound like a clown.

"You have a little girl," Ted said.

Melanie felt a lot better with the cool night air. "Yes," she said.

"Are you chilly? I could get a wrap from Mary Jo's room."

He knows Mary Jo's room and closet? "No, thanks," Melanie said, "my shawl is plenty, thanks. The air feels good. It was very warm in there."

"And getting sloppy," Ted said. "Some of these people arrived at six o'clock after an open house. One gentleman in particular needs to eat."

Melanie sipped and looked out over the knee-high stone wall. "This is lovely," she said. "I never knew this house was here."

"She had it built," Ted said. "Her own design. Mary Jo's flamboyant, but she does have a wonderful sense of materials."

"And décor," Melanie added. "There obviously isn't a child with jelly fingers allowed in that living room."

Ted laughed. "Would you rather go some place else to have dinner? Mary Jo won't care if we vanish."

"I think I better stay here." Melanie didn't think being alone with this young man an entire evening, going out to dinner alone, was exactly proper, certainly others wouldn't think so, either.

"Okay," Ted said. "If things get uncomfortable, give me a sign, and we'll disappear."

Melanie smiled. "Okay," she said. "Perhaps we better go back in now and mingle."

"After you," Ted said.

Mary Jo was in the center of a group of men who were obviously having fun with her. "There you are," she said when she spotted Melanie coming in through the patio doors. "Looking at the moon, were you? Come over here. There are way too many lecherous old men for me to handle."

As Mary Jo dragged her over to the swarm of older men, most of them old enough to be her grandfather, Melanie looked back. That offer of Ted's for a one-on-one evening sounded better all the time. About the fourth time one of Mary Jo's "lecherous old men" tried to hug and kiss Melanie, she set her drink down on a nearby tray and went looking for Ted. She found him leaning against the patio door, watching. "I'll take you up on that offer now," she said. "I've had more than enough."

No one really noticed them leaving, not even Mary Jo who was busy, not so much fending off potential lovers as redirecting their energies, looking around for someone to introduce.

So happy to be out of there, Melanie didn't really think about being in a car at night with a strange man. He suggested going to the Lodge, a restaurant on the outskirts of town, and though Melanie thought it was too expensive —she had never been, but she heard talk—it was also out of town and unlikely that they would be seen by anyone she knew.

It came as a big surprise to Melanie that people could afford such an expensive night out. She had not eaten out since before Edward left for the Army, almost five years now. She felt slightly guilty but more excited to be there, being served food she'd never eaten before. Ted insisted that she try the squab, something she never would have ordered with Gem. Or rabbit, or duck, or… there were so many things on the menu that would have caused her daughter to run out of the restaurant if she saw them on a plate.

"I hope you enjoy it," Ted said as their dinners were

served. "I had dinner here my first night in town and thought it was excellent."

"How long have you been here?"

"Three weeks. I'm settled in now and trying to get a feel for the area. I drive up and down looking at properties. Some mansions, some very nice homes like yours, and then some... not so nice. Typical of most American cities. Not too many for sale. Sign of the times."

"Aren't they predicting a boom in home sales with..." she stopped. She was going to say "with the men in service returning home", but the words stuck in her mouth. Her thoughts ran to Edward and suddenly the room, the candlelight, the wine, the fancy dinner, even the squab, left a bad taste in her mouth.

"You want to talk about your husband?" Ted asked. It was kind. He was kind, Melanie thought. "I don't think so," she said, putting down her fork.

"I'm sure he would want you to enjoy your meal."

Melanie sipped her wine. Once she settled down again, looked around the room, saw the people laughing and enjoying the evening, she felt guilty that the man across the table from her had spent so much money on this meal. She picked up her fork again. He thankfully changed the subject. "Tell me about your art."

She laughed slightly. "My cartoons," she said, self-deprecatingly.

"Your art," he repeated. "It is art. Where do you get your ideas?"

"It's fantasy."

"Is this a fantasy of yours? Are you a rescuer, a Woman Warrior?"

Melanie looked at him. "I never thought about myself that way," she admitted, "but now that you mention it, I suppose it is my fantasy. I want to save the world. I want to make everything right and happy... again." Everything they talked about came back to Edward. "Tell me about you," she said, taking another bite. The potatoes and vegetables were excellent. And the salad. She covered up the squab as best she could. Ted started talking about Cleveland, where he lived before. Melanie doubted that he noticed the amount of squab still on her plate when the waiter asked if he could remove it. Probably, he did.

He ordered cherries jubilee, which they flamed at the table. *Gem would love that.*

Ted's tale of his life in Cleveland was very interesting and ended the dinner on just the right amount of lightheartedness. He was one of seven children. *Seven!* One girl and six boys. Two of the boys had joined the Army and were planning on making it a career. One was a marine. Ted had joined the Navy. He said he was sorry that his health had not permitted him to see battle, but an asthmatic condition prevented him from active service. He received a medical discharge and returned home even before he completed basic training. He looked fit, about six feet tall, lean and muscular, Melanie thought. Although his suit coat hid his upper arms and chest, he had very broad shoulders and a slim waist, slim from the waist down, actually. She moved her eyes up to his eyes, green, sparkling, or was that the candlelight? *Eyes don't sparkle. Had to be the candlelight.*

They ended the dinner with coffee. Ted asked if she would like an after dinner drink, which she declined. The wine had given her a feeling of warmth all over. As they left the table, Ted put Melanie's shawl around her shoulders. It was hardly any touch at all, but his hands on her shoulders gave Melanie a sensation that was both intoxicating and frightening. She looked around quickly to be sure no one had seen.

The ride home was equally unnerving. Ted insisted on walking her to the door and waiting until she got inside before returning to the car.

He said, "Goodnight."

She thanked him. Twice.

Gem and Fred were asleep, Fred had the door to the guest room ajar, probably so he could hear Gem if she called to him. He was snoring. Melanie closed the door quietly, went into Gem's room and pulled the covers up around her little bare shoulders. She stirred, but did not awaken.

Melanie went downstairs to make sure that everything was secure. A final look around and then she went up to her room to undress. She hung up the dress, looked around for her shawl and realized that she didn't have it. It must have slipped off her shoulders in the car. Very quietly, she went back downstairs and looked out the front door. Ted's car was gone. He would find the shawl either when he got home or the next morning. And, he would return it. She would see him again.

Communion

Chapter Twenty-One

In the morning, Melanie made pancakes. She was just serving Fred when the doorbell rang. "I'll get it," Melanie said, as she put the skillet back on the stove. "The syrup's warm, Fred." She placed a small saucepan of melted butter on an oven mitt on the table. "Be careful, Gem. That pan is hot."

They were both busy eating when Melanie answered the door. She was pretty sure she knew who it was.

Ted was standing there with her shawl. He was dressed casually, jeans and a sweater. She'd been right about what she suspected were muscles. Very pronounced.

Asthma had not prevented him from developing like an athlete.

"I am so sorry you had to drive over here with my shawl," Melanie said.

"I don't know why I didn't see it when you went inside," Ted said. "Or, maybe I did and thought it was a good excuse to…"

Melanie realized that he had just seen something behind her. She turned. Fred and Gem were standing in the doorway of the kitchen. "Come here," Melanie said. "Come say hello to Mr. Baxter."

Fred came ahead; Gem behind him. "Come here, Sweetheart. Shake hands with Mr. Baxter."

She wouldn't.

"Hello, Gem."

"And this is my father-in-law, Fred Commons." The men shook hands.

"Mr. Commons," Ted said. "Have you lived in Erieville very long?"

"All my life," Fred said.

"Then you're just the man I'm looking for. Could I prevail upon you to ride around with me while I get acquainted with the town? There are so many similar sounding street names, I get lost every time I try to find my way."

"Mr. Baxter's in real estate," Melanie explained. "He's an agent in Mary Jo's company."

"I'm just having my breakfast," Fred said.

"Come in, Ted... Mr. Baxter," Melanie said. "Would you like some pancakes?"

"Just a cup of coffee would be great," Ted said. He closed the door behind him and followed Gem, who was looking back as she held Fred's hand into the kitchen.

Gem went outside, refusing to eat any more of the delicious pancakes. Fred helped himself to another serving of pancakes, butter and syrup. Ted joined Melanie in a cup of coffee. "Great sun porch and back yard," he mentioned, walking over and looking out. He saw Gem glance back at him, then run inside a playhouse that was partially constructed and disappear from his view, although he had the distinct feeling that she was watching him.

"I'm not taking you away from your work, am I, Fred?" Ted said, turning back to the table.

"Nope. And I'm finished here. Good breakfast, daughter."

"Thanks, Fred. More coffee, Mr. Baxter?"

"No, thanks. Call me Ted."

"All right."

Melanie followed Fred and Ted as they walked to the front door. "What if Abbey calls?" Melanie said.

"She won't."

The two men got into the car. Fred laughed at something Ted said, something Melanie didn't overhear—men stuff, she imagined. They were gone for over an hour. When Melanie heard the car pull into the drive, she looked out the front window. Fred got out of Ted's car, waved at him, got into his own, and they drove off. *Wonder how that went.*

Surprisingly, Ted Baxter was never mentioned again. Melanie was sure the name would come up the next time Fred stopped by, but it didn't. And Ted didn't call. Not that Melanie expected him to, but she thought there might be some... then it occurred to her: she was the one who owed him a thank you.

Gem was at school. Melanie sat at her drawing table in the sun porch and picked up her pens. She created Warrior Woman coming to the aid of a damsel-in-distress being chased by salivating overweight male pursuers. It was very funny. Melanie had drawn the damsel-in-distress in a black dress, with a fringed shawl dragging along behind her. She found an envelope and sent it to Ted Baxter at Mary Jo's Realty Company with a message that said simply, "a damsel-in-distress thanks you for a wonderful rescue."

The evening the call came through, Melanie was fortunately at home finishing up some work and listening to the radio. The phone didn't ring often in Melanie's house, hardly ever in the evening, so it was with an anxious feeling that she answered it.

"Hello?"

"Mrs. Commons? This is General O'Brien calling from France." It was so clear Melanie thought at first that it was a prank, but the General's voice was clear as a bell.

"General! What a wonderful surprise!"

"So happy to find you at home. How are things in my favorite new town?"

"Just fine. Fred is taking good care of your house."

"Good. And you, and your daughter?"

"We're both doing just fine, thank you."

"Are you up for some travel?"

"Pardon me? I'm not sure I heard you right."

"I'm sure you did. Would it be convenient for you and your daughter to hop on a plane and come to France?"

Melanie was so taken back, she couldn't answer.

"Is that a yes?"

"Are you serious?"

"Of course. I never joke about serious issues. I'll have a driver pick you up, make sure you get on the plane okay, and someone will meet you in Paris."

"Paris?"

"It will probably mean a change of planes in New York. I'm working on that now. How is the day after tomorrow, Wednesday?"

Too shocked to find her voice, for a few seconds Melanie just stood there in the kitchen unable to move.

"Still there? Haven't fainted, I hope."

"Does this mean you have some word about Edward?" Melanie finally dared to ask.

"I don't want to get your hopes up. I only have information about where their battalion was last heard from behind enemy lines. The countryside is strewn with debris from the bombs, some of them ours I'm afraid. Don't raise the hopes of your daughter. I have no idea who I'm looking for. He certainly wouldn't have been traveling under his American ID for the past three years. He may be greatly changed if he survived at all or if he went underground with the French. You should know that. You might tell your daughter that you're coming on a vacation."

"I think she'd see right through that," Melanie said. "She points to the spot on our world globe where her daddy may be."

"That's the word, I'm afraid, 'may'. If you won't get too disheartened walking through the villages where he and his unit went down…"

"I'd be *doing* something," Melanie said. "I've felt so helpless since..."

"Righto. That's my thinking as well. This was once beautiful countryside. Will be again some day. They're rebuilding already. Care to have a look?"

"Oh, yes!" Melanie heard herself shout through the phone. "I definitely want to have a look."

"Good!" Your tickets will be waiting for you at the airport in Cleveland. I'll have a driver pick you up at…"—pause—oh five hundred hours Wednesday."

"That's five in the morning, is it?"

He laughed. "Correct. Bring some warm clothes. It gets chilly at night."

"I don't know how to thank you."

"Poppyrot. None of that. How's your good friend, the realtor?"

"Asking about you."

"Good. Tell her… Never mind. I'll tell her when I return. See you in Paris, my dear. Adieu."

Melanie stood there in her kitchen with the phone in

her hand, the dial tone in her ear trying to think of what to do first. She almost dialed Mary Jo to tell her what the General said, but decided against letting anyone know where she and Gem were going.

Fred. Must get in touch with Fred to watch the house. And Gem's school. And where did she put that suitcase? Shouldn't she get a new one? She grabbed her purse, made sure she had change for the bus and headed to town. If she would be carrying a full suitcase in and out of airports, she could lug an empty one home on the bus.

There was no holding down Gem. When she arrived home after school, Melanie told her that they were going on a plane, just the two of them, on vacation. The child's eyes grew wide. When she ran to the globe and carried it over to the table pointing at Germany, Melanie's eyes misted. Of course, that would be where Gem wanted to go.

Chapter Twenty-Two

Along with a medium sized suitcase which both she and Gem would share, Melanie bought a small red purse for Gem to use for her essentials. Gem filled it with a trading card of a dog, a pocket flashlight that Fred had given her, one of Melanie's hankies, a very small doll from a long ago abandoned doll house, a locket with her picture and one of her father which Santa brought and a few other treasures, odds and ends, which held a special place in her heart.

Gem's little purse was on top of the suitcase in the entry very early Wednesday morning. At Melanie's insistence, the little girl managed to swallow three bites of oatmeal and half a glass of orange juice before she sat on top of the suitcase holding onto her little purse and waited.

Fred and even Abigail had stopped by the evening before to say goodbye. Abigail was rigid as she awkwardly returned the child's hug when they were leaving. Fred was too teary to let the child see. He picked her up, kept his face turned and jostled her awhile, up and down, up and down until he could regain his composure. If Abigail had the slightest thought that they would locate Edward, she didn't offer anything encouraging. She had given up all hope, certainly, harboring none of her grand daughter's faith.

The car was right on time the next morning. It was cool, clear skies promising perfect weather for flying. Melanie and Gem walked behind the chauffeur as he carried the suitcase to the car. Gem carried her own little purse and hung onto it for dear life in the car.

The trees were turning color as they drove through pastures and countryside, small towns whose occupants were just turning on lights and whose day, uneventful as the occupants of the chauffeured car, had begun. The list that Melanie made for herself had been checked over and over in the last day and a half. Six comic strips that Melanie had the foresight to prepare months before, getting ahead whenever the inspiration struck, were sent to Mr. Meyer to cover the upcoming weeks, along with a note stating that Melanie would be out of town for awhile. She would call upon her return. It would certainly not be even six weeks before they returned, she thought. The General hadn't mentioned a return date. Obviously, he didn't know himself. He had no idea *if* they would find... or *what* they would find... and certainly no idea *how long* the journey to discover Edward's whereabouts would last.

The night before as she was in bed and Melanie was tucking her in, Gem insisted on sleeping with her purse. "You know, sweetheart," Melanie said, "we'll be looking for your father and maybe the three of us—you, me and General O'Brien—will find someone who knows where he is." She kissed Gem's forehead. "And maybe we won't," she added softly. "But we'll try, won't we?"

The look on her daughter's face that night said it all. It was one of courage and something else. Confidence? Melanie didn't want to see that look change. What if they had to get back on the plane in Paris with no news at all? What if the little girl with the brave and confident look came back without her father? Looking at her now, smiling as she closed her eyes when Melanie turned out the light, Melanie felt caught up in that never wavering faith of her daughter's that her daddy would come home some day.

Gem expressed it in so many ways. His stocking on the mantle at Christmas. An empty space Gem insisted upon in the pew at church. Faith like that would surely not go unrewarded.

Surely.

The metropolis of Cleveland loomed in the distance. Gem was glued to the window staring out at the tall buildings and the size of the city. So many people were getting on airplanes at such an early hour, even though it was only seven o'clock (oh seven hundred hours, Melanie reminded herself) when they passed through the line. Finding their seats was an experience for both of them. Melanie had flown that time to New York to sign the contracts with the Hearst papers, and once before on a trip to Kentucky when her father died, her mother long since gone to her rest.

But this was luxury. A stewardess made Gem's comfort the most important thing she had to do that morning—pillows, blankets, coloring books and crayons, head sets for music. "Anything else I can get you, angel? Orange juice?" Gem smiled and shook her head. When Gem turned to look out the window, Melanie pointed to her mouth, then to Gem and shook her head. The stewardess got the message. She smiled, nodded, and sighed.

They landed in New York in what seemed like minutes, then off the plane and directed by the attentive stewardess to a gate in a different terminal. Melanie's bag had been checked through so, except for Gem's purse, they were free to walk unencumbered through the terminals until they found the international one with service to Paris. Only a few people were sitting around waiting to board. There was time for Melanie to pick up some reading material and a couple of candy bars in case they got hungry.

Hungry? From the time they stepped onto the plane until they landed in Paris, France almost eight hours later, all they did was eat and occasionally dose. Gem was entirely too excited to sleep. They managed to walk to the restrooms twice during the trip and back to their seats without falling on top of anyone, although the turbulence which jostled them made walking and climbing over other passengers interesting indeed.

They were served dinner, but Gem was too excited to eat. And snacks. That she managed. And drinks. Seven-up. And coloring books for Gem, but mostly she stared out at the clouds. The clouds fascinated Gem. She would tug on her mother's sleeve and point out the window when they passed through or over or under or around a particularly unusual bank of clouds.

The descent was a bit painful. Gem held her ears and looked at her mother. "Swallow, sweetheart," Melanie said, swallowing herself. "It'll be over soon."

The prospect of arriving in a foreign country, one in which she could not speak the language, scared Melanie to death, but she had to pretend that she knew exactly where to go and what to do. It was dark; there was very little to see out the window of the plane. Before they got off, a stewardess and even the pilot came out of the cockpit to give Gem her wings, a little set of silver wings for her sweater, which he pinned on her. Then, he saluted her and Gem returned the salute.

"What an angel you are," he said. "Come fly with us again, will you now that you have your wings? Or, perhaps you don't need a plane to fly."

Gem smiled and shrugged. *Maybe she didn't. She was like a bird.*

A man in uniform approached them as soon as they stepped inside the terminal. "Mrs. Commons?"

"Yes."

"This way, please. We have a car waiting."

Her first time abroad, Melanie expected everything to be different, but people looked the same. And although she heard a language she could only admire but not understand, they really didn't talk with each other in all that different a manner. They dressed the same, were in the same terrible hurry to get to where they were going, and were, as people are everywhere, terribly impatient to get there.

Melanie gave the uniformed man her ticket for her suitcase which he retrieved at the carousel where all of the luggage was coming through on a conveyor.

The crowd, the people rushing past, and the language frightened Gem. She looked up at her mother more than once. "Would you like me to carry you?" Melanie asked, but Gem shook her head no. They had to walk quickly to keep up with the crowd.

It would never be like this again, Melanie thought as the uniformed man opened the door of a car at the curb when they walked outside. A car waiting at curbside, someone to retrieve your luggage and whisk you out of the airport was not everyone's manner of travel. Melanie reminded herself to thank the General for the special attention when they caught up with him, whenever that might be.

The ride through Paris was exciting. They didn't pass any landmarks that Melanie would have recognized, like the tower or the arch. They seemed to be on the outskirts, in a very nice, very quiet part of the city. The driver pulled up in front of a marquee with lettering in French. The doorman quickly opened the car door. "Bonjour, Madam."

Not trusting her French, all of it learned from books, Melanie said, "Good... evening." She knew their driver spoke English. "What time is it, please?" Melanie asked.

"Sixteen hundred hours, Madam," he responded.

Melanie shook her watch. "Eight hours difference, Madam."

"Oh. Of course." How stupid of her. "Thank you."

"I'll take you to the front desk. Your room has been reserved."

Fortunately, the driver and the desk clerk conversed in French. Whatever they said, Melanie took the pen from the clerk, who smiled and bowed. She signed their names, then the clerk handed the driver a key.

The driver saw them to their rooms, opened the door with the key, turned on the light, made sure the room was secure and said, "Have a good stay, Mrs. Commons. I'll see you in the morning."

"Not too early I hope," Melanie said.

"Eleven o'clock, the General said," he responded.

"Have a good evening." He left them.

Oh, dear, Melanie thought. Alone in Paris. She locked the door with the bolt and chain and yawned. "Let's get to sleep, sweetheart. Sweetheart?" For a few seconds, Melanie panicked until she found Gem standing in the enormous bathroom with a shower, black and white tile floor and the fluffiest white towels Melanie had ever seen in her life.

Gem looked around, looking for *it*, Melanie suddenly realized. "There's only a shower, dear. No tub." Gem didn't understand, but Melanie said, "We'll shower when we wake up. Right now, we need sleep." They undressed and put on their nightgowns. Melanie hung up their clothes, turned around to ask Gem if she brushed her teeth and found her sound asleep clutching her purse under the covers.

Communion

Chapter Twenty-Three

From the moment she abruptly awakened with the sun pouring through the windows until they arrived downstairs in the lobby at one minute before the scheduled time, having enjoyed a complimentary Continental breakfast delivered to their room and showered—both of them together in the luxurious warmth of the glass and chrome enclosure—Melanie wondered how they would get along not speaking the language.

General O'Brien in full uniform, one star on each of his shoulders, was waiting for them. He was speaking with the desk clerk conferring over a map and pointing. He was speaking in English and having a hard time being understood, giving up actually as Melanie and Gem stepped out of the elevator.

"Welcome to Paris," he said in that booming voice of his. "Had breakfast, have you?"

"Yes, thank you. Thank you for everything. We are so spoiled. Gem will think traveling is always this comfortable."

"Sergeant Miller's a good man, very conscientious. Treated you like his own family, I'm sure."

"Exactly like that. Even nicer," Melanie said, smiling.

"Our little girl looks like she's ready to go." And with that, Gem put her purse in her right hand and took the General's hand in her left. "All right then," he said. "We're off."

Again, a car stood at attention curbside, only this time it was a military van with the insignia of the United States Army on the side, with Sergeant Miller at the wheel. He came around abruptly to open the passenger door for Melanie and Gem. The General hopped into the front seat.

"Beautiful morning," Melanie remarked when they were on their way.

"Yes," the General said. "You brought it with you. It's been raining for a week."

He took the map he'd folded earlier out of his inside coat pocket and unfolded it.

"Reims, Miller."

"Yes, sir."

"We'll start there." He turned slightly to address Melanie. "This morning we'll see as much as possible of Reims. This part of France was lost to the Germans in 1940 and returned a few months ago with the signing of the surrender document. The Act of Military Surrender was signed the next day in Berlin at the insistence of the Soviets. Now, France will occupy itself with rebuilding its cities. Many large projects have already begun, but the roads have paid the price for this war. I'm afraid with the rain, some of the roads may be washed out, certainly muddy."

He consulted the map. "We're unlikely to learn anything in Reims itself, Miller. Stop along the way if you see a town where we might look around and inquire about an American soldier."

"Yes, sir."

"A needle in a haystack, I'm afraid, my dear, but we know that Edward's battalion was driven back behind the German border in the Alsace region. This is as good a place as any to begin. You won't get discouraged, I hope, if we strike out mostly."

"I won't; I promise," Melanie said, knowing she couldn't prevent it. She dared not hope that they would be directed exactly to where they would find Edward in this vast bombed out haystack.

It was anything but a tourist's stop, what with the ruble in the streets. Bulldozers had already begun their work, but now sat idle until the effects of the storm were over. "I thought we might have lunch here," General O'Brien said, "but it's worse than I feared. Let's drive awhile, Miller."

"Yes, Sir."

"Hard to believe, isn't it," General O'Brien said as he looked at the ruined Cathedral and government buildings. "This might have been any American city if we'd not prevailed. Too horrible to contemplate." He appeared to be talking to himself, not to anyone particular in the car. Melanie looked over at Gem to make sure she wasn't alarmed by the sights, but she had fallen asleep, for which Melanie was grateful. The road was unpaved, deeply rutted, bouncing them around, forcing Melanie to hang onto the strap in one hand and her daughter in the other. And still, Gem slept. Or, at least, her eyes were closed.

The towns were heavily damaged, ruble

everywhere, skeletons of what they once were. They drove another hour before they came upon a small town, green hillside, buildings obviously overlooked by the Luftwaffe or the Americans in search of factories and munitions. Sheep herders and wool gatherers seemed to be the main occupation of the small town. The General spied what looked like a French café where a few patrons were sitting outside. "Here," he said.

They must have been a strange looking lot. A one star General, a sergeant, a young American woman and a child. No one would forget, if asked, that this group of strangers came asking about an American soldier. Did they know of any American soldiers in the area? While the sergeant inquired, the General, Melanie and Gem went inside to order cheese, croissants and fruit which they decided to take with them since seating was sparse and the Frenchmen sitting around did not look all that friendly.

The four returned to the car where they ate their lunch. "Let's drive on ahead," General O'Brien said. "I could use a strong cup of coffee."

The General decided that the town of Metz, their next destination, was too far to aim for in the daylight remaining to them. After consulting the map, he decided that they should stop at the next reasonably clean inn they could find.

What they located half an hour later was not even on the map. A town without a name. There was just one street, a building with rooms, which appeared clean, and featured a small restaurant next door. "Perfect," the General said. He registered them into three rooms and told the attendant behind the desk that they would reconnoiter at oh seven hundred hours. The attendant stared at him. General O'Brien turned over the translation to Miller who, in impeccable French, relayed the General's message to the man behind the desk. The man then handed Miller three keys.

The remaining daylight hours were spent walking through the small town inquiring about American soldiers in the area. Mostly they got blank stares in response.

"I think they're wary, General," Sergeant Miller said after several encounters. "They may think they'll be arrested if the Americans we're looking for have deserted."

"Deserted!" barked General O'Brien. "You mean they..." He looked back at the small group of men huddled together, watching, and whispering. "You're right. I see that now. Why else would a General be out looking for his soldiers. The war is over." He shook his head. "Big mistake, Miller. I should have realized. Let's go back to the inn."

After a short rest and bath—Gem was happy to see a tub again—Melanie and Gem came downstairs to join their soldiers. Melanie almost didn't recognize them. The General was wearing an Irish cable knit sweater over a collared shirt, corduroy pants and half boots. Sergeant Miller was wearing jeans and a turtleneck. "Now we'll fit in with the others," the General said. "Let's eat. I'm famished."

It was an excellent meal. In this town, they would be remembered as the General and his party, but the next day and the days thereafter as they moved around, it was hoped they would be regarded with less fear.

It was tested the next morning. They left the small town where they stayed just after breakfast and drove for nearly two hours before coming upon a small village on the road to Metz. "Sir," Miller pointed out. "The insignia on the car."

"And what do you propose I do about that, Miller? This isn't exactly a mecca with a rental car company on every corner."

"I thought perhaps we could leave the car half a mile or so from town and stroll in as tourists on holiday."

"You expect this lady and her child to…"

"We don't mind," Melanie broke in. "I'm wearing

comfortable shoes and Gem loves to walk."

"I could carry her piggyback," Miller suggested. The General appeared embarrassed that he hadn't thought of the idea himself.

They set out on foot leaving the car in a secluded area, but where they could certainly find it again once they had decided to move on. Melanie and the General were hampered by their lack of French in asking about an American soldier, so Sergeant Miller made the inquiries. People didn't seem nearly so reluctant to talk to him, but after a dozen or more stops, Melanie became quite tired of seeing shop keepers shake their heads and respond, "Non."

After three such villages they arrived in the town of Metz. It was a large enough town that they were able to park the car in a garage and travel around town on foot. "You should know, my dear," the General told Melanie, that your husband was a member of the 716th Battalion whose critical assignment it was to restore rail cars confiscated by the Germans and return them to France where there was a desperate need. The men of the 716th Battalion had been involved in major bombings when the rail yards at Sablon were destroyed by the Germans."

"Was Edward…?"

"I'm afraid this is where communications break

down. But, if he'd been killed, there would be information. Or, even taken prisoner, we would know it. In this case, no news is good news. That's why we're here, isn't it. I just wanted you to know what an important role your husband and his battalion played in the war. Let's move on, shall we? Let us know if you get tired, little one."

As she insisted on doing with each new town they entered, Gem took the General's hand and kept up with him. It wasn't hard to see how much that pleased the straight backed, handsome elder man out for a stroll with his granddaughter, daughter, and her husband. It was obvious, wasn't it?

They learned nothing in Metz. Melanie's feet did ache though she tried not to show her discomfort. One curious thing occurred. It was while they were stopped at a sidewalk café for a coffee. Gem had a sweet roll.

Miller and the General were going over the map looking for towns bordering Metz. Melanie was checking her Berlitz French for Beginners to try to improve her pronunciation of some basic French words when several birds appeared begging for crumbs. Gem proceeded to toss them the remnants of her roll. She was soon out of crumbs but the birds kept chirping away, walking up to her, walking away, walking back to her, walking away. Melanie was used to birds acting strangely around her daughter, but that was at home in their surroundings with birds that became familiar with daily routines and in their back yard where they might find a nibble or two left over from a tea party.

Melanie watched for several minutes. Without anyone moving, the birds flew up to a pole, then down on the ground again, surrounding Gem, then back to the top of the pole, circling it before landing on the perch. Then, they flew to the next pole. After pausing for a moment sure that the pattern had been noticed, they then flew back and repeated the whole cycle once more. After two or three times through the pattern, Gem started to follow them.

"Gem," her mother said, once she realized what she was doing. "Stay here."

But the birds flew down beside Gem, landed at her feet, chirped loudly, and then jumped away heading east, landing on the next pole farther off in the distance where they stopped and waited. Gem looked at her mother and pointed in their direction.

Why in the world she said what she did, Melanie would wonder later. "If there is a choice," she said to the General who was studying the map with Miller, "may I suggest that we go east."

Both Miller and the General looked at her. "What?"

"That way," Melanie said, pointing. She couldn't come out and say that the birds were beckoning to her little girl because she had this way of communicating with birds —most animals actually—and Melanie found that over the years such non verbal messages should not be ignored. There was a... network, she had come to realize, for lack of a better description, a communion that few humans were privileged to access, but to her dying day she would attest that her daughter was one of those privileged few who broke through. It had been there from the beginning, Melanie realized as she watched the birds and her daughter interact. There had been the deer in the back of the garden who led Gem safely out of the woods; the cat and the squirrel on the windowsill; the birds in the yard. What the family had come to accept as commonplace was not common at all.

How quickly, Melanie thought, had they assimilated this phenomenon into their everyday existence, accepting it as normal when it was anything but normal. Had they been afraid to admit to themselves or others that their child was different? Would exploring this gift, or curse, be admitting that there was something unusual about their child, something beyond explanation? Something frightening?

In that place at that moment in the courtyard of a small French café, Melanie suddenly understood that her little girl was not, as she feared, possessed, but possessed extraordinary powers to communicate non-verbally with creatures big and small.

At Melanie's request to continue their journey to the east, the General and the Sergeant looked at each other in such a way that Melanie was certain they felt that she was daft. East lay the city of Strasbourg, a German stronghold until it fell to the French, an unlikely place to find an American soldier, alive. Melanie continued to watch the birds walking and flying off a short distance, always returning to Gem, who was standing by the little round table outside the cafe. All Melanie knew was that she felt something, something she would never be able to identify or describe to anyone.

Would the General and Sergeant Miller mind very much retrieving the car and meeting them here? She appeared to have developed a blister on her toe.

Gem looked at her mother with a half smile.

So it was that the little group headed east out of Metz, stopping to ask directions at the next small town. Gem and Melanie watched for the birds who were perched on top of wires leading out of town. The birds flew east again. "May we go on?" Melanie suggested knowing full well that she had no credence for what she was asking and it was getting late. They would have to return to the hotel soon if they wanted to get back before dark. "Please," Melanie heard herself ask. Gem took General O'Brien's hand in both of hers. She looked up at him. He saw her form the word with her lips. "Please."

They were back in the car. It made no sense to keep going east. The General turned to look into the back seat once. Gem was looking out the window, up at the wires. Miller glanced at the General, shrugged, and drove on.

A small town not on the map, two streets long, appeared up ahead a hundred yards from where the General was just about to take a stand and tell Miller to turn around.

Gem glanced at her mother. She held her two hands together, steepled, then crossed fingers.

When they got out of the car at the end of the street, Melanie looked up. The birds had perched on the pole. They were not moving on. General O'Brien and Sergeant Miller tried to follow her glance skyward but could not see what she saw, as though it was written in the sky, and Melanie thought, *maybe it was*. The birds had definitely perched where they were.

"I'll take this side of the street," Melanie said. "I

think I can say, 'Have you seen an American?' now without embarrassing myself too badly."

Melanie and Gem walked quickly ahead. It was getting dark. They barely had time, Melanie realized, as she walked into a market to inquire. And again the answer, "Non." No American.

When Melanie walked outside she realized that Gem was not with her. "Gem!" she screamed. "Gem!"

General O'Brien looked around, taking in the small town in one glance. "Where did she go?"

"I don't know. She was right here when I went into the market."

"Maybe she's..." Sergeant Miller started to say when Melanie looked farther down the street.

"There," she said. "That's where she'll be." She ran, forgetting the purported blister on her toe.

The General and Sergeant Miller hurried to catch up. They could smell the place before they saw it. The wonderful aroma of bread and buns surrounded them even before they entered the little shop with the bell overhead.

"Gem!" Melanie called.

"A little girl—Un petite cher," Sergeant Miller said to the man behind the counter. The man pointed to a curtained door.

Melanie darted inside. It led to a covered patio. And there, staring down at a man sitting at a table rolling out dough, was Gem, tears streaming down her face.

"Gem."

She didn't turn around.

Communion

Chapter Twenty-Four

Sergeant Miller took the baker aside. He seemed reluctant at first to talk about the man he had harbored during the war, but when Sergeant Miller pointed out, in French, that they were only there to reunite a prisoner of war with his family, and the baker's identity would be protected, though his heroism would be rewarded by the United States Government, the man started talking excitedly.

He said that the poor soldier who sat before them had arrived a year earlier, dressed in the assembled uniforms of British and American soldiers. He had a large scar running down the side of his face and a ghostly stare.

There were dark rings around his eyes, the baker said, and thin, red veins streaming upwards to his hairline. He didn't speak so much as moan, and the baker gave him a croissant and a glass of water out of pity. The soldier came back every day for a week, and every day he was given a croissant and water.

The town had been largely ignored by the Nazis after France fell, but periodically they would come through, and the baker worried what would happen if anyone saw him feeding an Allied soldier. He didn't want the man to starve, so he offered him a job in the bakery. The man seemed, for the first time, to cheer up. The baker wasn't sure how to communicate with the man, but after demonstrating how to sweep and organize the storefront, the man seemed to understand and performed the tasks exactly as he had been taught. He was also given some old clothes to better fit in with the locals.

One day, a cadre of Nazis came through and stopped at the bakery. They inquired about the gangly man with the odd appearance who refused to talk. The baker said it was his son, who was mentally "touched" and hadn't spoken since he was a child. The ruse worked, but the baker decided it would be best to give the man a back of the house position. Just as he had caught on how to sweep and assemble the storefront after a single instruction, so too did he learn how to bake an assortment of pastries with little instruction.

The baker noticed that, when he initially brought out the dough to demonstrate its preparation, the man seemed to come alive. He stood more upright, his eyes became animated, and when he was finally able to touch the dough, a large smile brightened his previously drawn lips. He inferred the man must have been a baker prior to the war, and this arrangement proved considerably profitable, as word spread around town about the bakery and its phenomenal new pastry chef.

"And he's never spoken to you," Sergeant Miller asked after the baker related the story to him.

"Non." In French, he said, "Not a single word. Although I noticed early on a rather strange thing. Animals seem to follow him."

"Follow him?"

"Yes, birds especially, and occasionally dogs. I saw a rat standing next to him in the kitchen one day, but it wasn't scurrying around, it sat next to his foot and just looked at him, and if I weren't of sound mind, I'd say that he was talking to it. Either way, he was visibly upset when I told him he couldn't bring any animals into the bakery, especially not rats. But no, not a single word. I only know his name from his dog tags, Edward Commons."

"Does he stay with you?"

"I have an apartment upstairs that I rented out before the war. He sleeps there but he doesn't have any personal items. The only clothes he has are ones my wife gives him, mostly from our son, who died when the Germans invaded. Strange as he is, he's become a member of our family."

As Miller and the baker spoke, Edward sat in the back of the kitchen, surrounded by General O'Brien and Melanie. Gem had perched herself on his lap, and although he had accepted the gesture, it was passive. While his gaze never met hers, Gem's eyes were transfixed on him. Melanie wasn't sure if she should hug him, since he seemed not to recognize her. His distant gaze, his limp posture, and his unresponsiveness, though not a direct rejection, was alarming enough to keep her growing desire at bay to seize him in her arms and cover him in kisses.

Still, it gnawed at her. She had imagined this moment for nearly four years. She had mapped every nuance of his face, the first time he'd see her, choreographed their mad dash to each other, and had tasted his kiss in dream after dream for four interminable years.

She had rejected suitors, been rejected by his mother, raised a now-mute child, started a career, all with the hopes that this sacred moment would come true.

Instead, her reality was an old bakery in a small town in Northeastern France, her knight in shinning armor reduced to a sullen mass of flesh and bone, who did not recognize his own family, and who, much like their daughter, refused to speak.

"Edward," Melanie said, "Edward, I'm your wife. This child is your daughter, Gemini. Gem. Our home is in Erieville, Ohio. In America. A small town, not too different from this one. I'm an artist. Do you remember, Edward? You and your father built me an art studio in your parent's house, where we lived. You worked at the Montgomery Bakery on the edge of town, near Lake Kashuma where you used to take me before we got married. The same lake where one evening you took me to watch the full moon rise above the trees, and when it came up over the branches, you handed me a hot cross bun, my favorite. You put a ring in the middle that almost chipped my tooth, but when I saw it I was too happy to care. There, you got on your knee and asked me to marry you. You reminded me of that night every time things were going bad in our life. You always said that when I said 'Yes', it was the happiest moment of your life, and the only thing that equaled it was the day Gem was born. Now, we're here; we're both here. We've come to take you home."

As she was talking, her hand had found its way to Edward's knee, and when she said "home" she instinctively squeezed it, inciting the first reaction he had given them since they showed up. He looked at her for the first time. He didn't smile; he didn't speak. He only looked. But, it was at her, and not at some indistinct point miles away, like he had been doing.

"We have our own home now, Edward. Your mother needed our room for a boarder, but she did us a favor, really. We have a lovely home. A wonderful home. I'm sure you can get your job back at the bakery. Everyone remembers you. I'm working at home now. I draw a comic strip which has become very popular."

She pulled out two prints she had folded in her purse. Edward looked at them for a moment and then back at Melanie.

"I draw at home. I make a good income from it, so you don't have to go back to work until you're ready. We have a good size kitchen. We can fix it up so you can have your own bake shop in the house. And Gem could help you. She'd love to work with you. We'd be a family again.

Wouldn't you like that? Edward?"

Edward's gaze shot toward the window across the room as two birds flew up and perched themselves on the outside railing. Melanie saw in his eyes that she had lost him again. General O'Brien saw the hurt in her face and touched her arm.

"Why don't you take Gem outside for a minute and let me talk to Edward? I think the poor boy is a bit overwhelmed."

With much effort, Gem was convinced to join Melanie outside, where Sergeant Miller relayed to her the story the baker told him.

"He clearly has shell shock," Sergeant Miller said. "He'll be debriefed and examined before he can return to civilian life."

"How long will that take?"

"Given the current situation, I can't say. Most likely we can complete it once we return to Paris. Hopefully, a few days. He's been through a very traumatic time."

While the adults spoke, Gem had become transfixed on a pair of birds standing by the corner of the bakery. She approached the birds and knelt down in front of them. One of the birds approached her, chirping and picking at the ground. She extended her forefinger and the bird rubbed it with the back of its head. She then scooped it up into her arms and clutched it to her chest. The bird cooed and when Gem loosened her grip it flew down the street, accompanied by its companion. Gem watched, content, as the birds soared through the sky, finally coming to rest on a balcony.

Gem looked over her shoulder at her mother, who was close to breaking down but somehow held onto her composure. Gem wrapped her arms around her mother's waist. Melanie, barely paying attention, instinctively caressed the back of her daughter's head. Before she realized that it was, in fact, her daughter who spoke, she heard, "Daddy loves us." For the first time in three years, her daughter spoke.

"Go home now," Gem said.

Melanie grabbed her and hugged her. All this time, she had been able to speak. She should be furious, Melanie thought, but she was so thrilled to hear her daughter's voice that all she could do was hug her. The General was standing in the doorway having heard everything. He reached into his pocket for his sunglasses.

Through a blur of tears—the release of emotion bottled up inside her since that dreadful day years before when the letter arrived—Melanie and Gem, along with the

General, Edward Commons and Sergeant Miller, shook hands with the baker, waved to his wife in an upstairs window and headed for the car. Edward turned to look back. Tears were shed by everyone, including the stunned young man himself who allowed the little girl named Gem and the woman who claimed to be his wife, to hold onto his hands and lead him away.

In the car, Gem opened up. She did not stop talking, whether about school or her toys, or about Warrior Woman, how she was led to the General's house by her friend, a doe named Margaret, everything that happened in the past four years it seemed until they reached Paris. General O'Brien was as shocked as everyone else in the car, unable to get in a word while Gem made up for lost years of talking. "She can outtalk me," he said once, interrupting, but not stopping the chatter.

Edward kept his eyes out the window of the car, the French countryside passing by, without any reaction, either of joy or pain. It was as though every image simply embedded itself on his pupil, rushing over the dark space interspersed by occasional blinking. The pockmarked road, which jostled the car every couple of minutes, didn't even register in his body, pinned as it was in his seat by sheer will and an indescribable sadness that emanated from his posture.

When Melanie had first seen him, he was in the middle of making crepes. The man she saw—confident, gentle, warm—faded the moment his attention was turned away from the task at hand. The longer they spoke to him, the more withered he became, and when he was told that he would no longer work at the bakery, the ghost-like stare the baker had described to Sergeant Miller crept back, the pale skin, the hollowed expression. Tears had streamed down his face when they first entered the car, although he did not sob audibly and his body did not convulse. He simply sat, allowing the tears to wet his face without interruption while his daughter spoke endlessly. At one point, Melanie thought, Gem might have grown weary, but it was only a pause, too short a pause for anyone else to break in. She was covering for her father.

"I know you're sad about leaving the bakery, daddy," Gem said, "but we have a wonderful kitchen at home. We'll get you eggs and flour, and I'll help you bake something, and mommy can help. We can bake as much as you want. Anything you want. Maybe we can get some blueberries and strawberries and you can show me how to make that thing you were making in the kitchen back there. What are those things called? They looked 'licious. You could teach me everything you learned here, and—"

Edward reached out for Gem's hand. Everyone in the car waited for some kind of response, maybe he'd smile, or maybe he'd finally talk. But, grabbing her hand was the only reaction he gave all day.

A few minutes later, they stopped at a small inn outside Paris. Edward stayed in a room with Sergeant Miller and General O'Brien. Gem wanted him to stay in their room, but the General explained that they needed to talk to her daddy. The next day, they arrived in Paris and the men departed, the General said they were going to the embassy to give Edward a debriefing and to ask him some questions. Melanie understood though she didn't try to explain it to Gem. The United States Army had to make sure that Corporal Edward Commons hadn't abandoned his post. They had to make sure he *could* return to civilian life, that her husband was the good and honorable man that she believed he was and would continue to be.

While the men were away, Melanie and Gem explored Paris, visiting shops, cafés and parks. The language barrier still made things difficult, but they found the Parisians to be much more accommodating than expected, no doubt due to leftover gratitude for Americans having liberated the city. Melanie was especially interested in the art galleries, and they found a few that were open. During these sprawling adventures across Paris, she told her daughter about the different styles, about the Impressionists, the Cubists, and the masters of the Renaissance. They found a gallery that had a Monet exhibit and Melanie nearly cried looking at the paintings, the elegant moments of a fading and elegaic world caught with movement and passion in a web of oil paints and thick brush strokes layered on a stretched canvas.

"Why are you sad, mommy?"

"Not sad, sweetheart, overjoyed. This was always my dream, to come here, to see these magnificent paintings."

After looking at famous artwork for nearly a week, Melanie took Gem to the Eiffel tower. They found a place to picnic nearby, and while Gem ate her sandwich, Melanie took out a sketch pad she had bought at one of the shops and began sketching the scene before her. Having spent the last few days immersed in European artwork, she found her images taking on a new form. It was still very much her style, but her angles were just slightly different, just enough to skew that Norman Rockwell style that had held her back in her pre-*Warrior Woman* days.

She also found that, having focused on comic-style

imagery the last couple of years, her aesthetic had become more iconic. Since *Warrior Woman* was her bread and butter, she had learned certain shorthand for images and characters, to make them at once accessible and easy to duplicate repeatedly. Her initial sketch of Gem was the stereotypical young American child, blond hair, fair skin, plump features. It was smooth and expressed the confidence she had developed over the last couple of years while making a life for herself and for Gem.

She was disgusted by it at first, though, feeling the effortlessness was a cheat, so she sketched her daughter again, this time focusing on small details, the way her fingers held the bread, the way her mouth curled at the edges when she ate, how her head fell forward causing her hair to sweep over her eyes. She focused on how upright her posture was. For a little girl, she sat like a woman, not even allowing her legs to spread out like most children. And another feature caught Melanie off-guard—how much Gem looked like her.

Consumed as she had been by her life during those past years, she hadn't thought about such things the last few years. Here, in Paris, at the end of their wait, at the moment of joy suspended while Edward was being debriefed and his fate decided, Melanie had a moment to exhale and see the world around her in a new and rejuvenated manner. Her eyes looked upon her daughter refreshed and recognized this beautiful life she had created with Edward. Gem was so much the epitome of her father, the strong work ethic, the gentle spirit, the inquisitiveness, and love of life, but her body, her face, the way she held herself: she was the spitting image of her mother.

As she sketched her daughter, Melanie felt a rush of love that had been lost on her since Gem was a baby. The last few years her love for her daughter was instinctive, and often protective, but she didn't enjoy the beauty of her the way she did when she was an infant. She had found that when she told people that Gem was her daughter, it was with a hint of apprehension, given Gem's eccentricities, but looking at her now, in this park, with the Eiffel Tower in the distance, eating a sandwich and clearly enjoying it, Melanie felt for the first time in years proud to be her mother. This little girl, she knew, could conquer the world.

And this little girl could also still surprise Melanie. As they approached their hotel, Gem stopped in the middle of the sidewalk and refused to move.

"Gem, what is it? What's wrong?"

"I love you, mommy."

"I love you, too, sweetheart."

"I'm sorry."

"For what?"

"For not speaking to you."

Ever since they were separated from the men, Melanie had inquired about why Gem hadn't talked for so long. At first, she had been upset, and it only made Gem cry. Then, she approached the subject more gently, but Gem would either change the subject or just look at the ground. Melanie felt that maybe the girl was ashamed, and hearing her now, she knew that she had been right.

"Baby, listen to me: life was hard before you were born, and whatever we've gone through the last few years, it wasn't because of you that things were hard. That's just life. You'll find as you get older that you can't control very much, but you can control how you deal with it. Now, I think we've done very well for ourselves, and I never, ever would have wanted to go through it without you. Okay?"

"Okay."

They held each other for a couple of minutes before pedestrian traffic became irritated by the roadblock they had created. Gem took her mother's hand and they continued on to the hotel. Perhaps, she'd never be able to explain to her mother why she hadn't talked all that time. Maybe one day she'd find a way to explain it, but either way, Melanie no longer felt that she needed an answer.

Chapter Twenty-Five

After three and a half weeks of exams, interviews, and meetings, Edward was honorably discharged and allowed to return to the States with his family. Although he wouldn't talk to anyone, it had been documented that his platoon had been largely killed off during a raid just twenty miles north of Metz. Only one other man had been found from his platoon, and he had reported that the raid had been so chaotic and brutal that when it was over he wasn't even sure where he was. It was two days before he came across a corpse that he could identify as having been one of the young men from his platoon. Those whose job it was to identify members of the platoon concluded that the same thing had happened to Edward Commons. Very likely, he would never be found alive.

When Melanie and Gem first saw Edward after he was discharged from the embassy, he seemed slightly more stable than when they met in the bakery. He didn't appear gaunt, although his eyes still possessed a sad, broken stare. He was quiet but more interactive, nodding or smiling when spoken to. Melanie worried what would happen when they returned home, how Abigail would take his condition. Fred, she felt, would understand, but Abigail might lash out, as she had to Gem all these years, and Melanie felt that defensive instinct kick in once more, ready to guard the man she loved.

It was a routine drive to the airport and the check-in went smoothly. The General in uniform, Melanie, Edward and Gem were in line to board. As they approached the gateway, Edward stopped and the silent tears from the other day began running. Melanie turned toward him and urged him along. When he didn't respond, Gem walked over to take his hand.

"Its okay daddy; it's safe."

Edward's lip began to tremble, fear emanating from his now livid eyes. He looked around the airport, and as he took in the last of France, the place he had called home for the past few years, he lost it. His silent tears turned into anguished sobs. He collapsed to his knees and wept uncontrollably. Gem tried to calm him, but Melanie swept her up as the General lifted Edward to his feet. Melanie tried to remove Gem, who was calling out to her father, while the General spoke sternly in his ear. After a couple of minutes, Edward relaxed, caved actually. They were able to board the plane without further incident.

For the first half of the flight, they sat quietly, Gem next to her daddy, the General and Melanie across from them at the bulkhead. When they were in the air, Gem opened her purse and handed her daddy a wrapped candy, a lemon drop like he used to bring her from the bakery.

Edward accepted the candy with a smile. Not long after, he fell asleep, followed by Gem, leaning on his shoulder. Melanie said to no one in particular, "She had to have brought that candy from home. She must have had it ever since he gave it to her, when he came home one afternoon from the bakery in town."

General O'Brien took Melanie's hand. "He's going to be all right, but it'll be a long struggle. You may want to consider a..." he chose his words carefully, "convalescent home for awhile."

"No. Absolutely not. I understand why you would

say that, but the last thing he needs is to be pawned off on somebody else. I'll take care of him. I didn't know what to expect before we came here, but now I know what needs to be done. We'll proceed slowly and cautiously."

"That's very caring of you."

"I do care."

"The doctors in Paris said he may not fully recover."

"They're wrong," Melanie said obstinately.

The General patted her hand and turned to look at the sleeping father and daughter across from him. If anyone could make it happen, he thought, if anyone could make love awaken in such a battered world full of wounded souls, these two strong women could.

Home.

The rest of the flight to Cleveland was quiet, but not uncomfortable. Edward seemed relaxed once they landed. As they drove past Cleveland, he even seemed to smile a little at the skyline. Seeing him this way relieved Melanie, who was beginning to feel the effects of jetlag and utter exhaustion. She dozed off in the chauffered car for what felt like just a few seconds, but had to be shaken awake by Gem as they pulled up in front of her house an hour later.

It was early morning. Melanie contemplated calling Fred, but her body told her no, today we rest. Edward and

Gem must surely be feeling as she was, she thought, overly tired and not thinking too clearly. It would be stressful enough getting Edward adjusted to the house without his parents confronting him with their embraces and questions, Abigail particularly. Time for that. Maybe, the day after. A phone call to Fred later, she thought, letting him know the situation, and insisting that they wait before seeing Edward. She would insist that Edward was in a very fragile state and request that they have the kindness to allow him to re-enter his home and his life in his time.

Melanie thanked and hugged the General, hugging him a long time. He helped bring their luggage inside and mentioned in passing—although Melanie thought that he was trying to add some levity to the emotional situation—that he wondered what Mary Jo might be up to that day. How he could think of seeing anybody while experiencing jet lag was beyond Melanie, but she was pleased to see him thinking about Mary Jo, a hopeful sign. A tired smile stumbled across her lips.

They barely arrived before Gem took her father by the hand and dragged him to the back yard to see her playhouse. Once Melanie had sorted out the luggage and placed the dirty clothes in the wash basket, she sat down and watched Gem serving tea to her bears and her father.

Gem was talking incessantly. Edward sat back and appeared to be listening, holding the cup close to him, like a treasure.

He was a handsome man. Melanie had forgotten how handsome, even after seeing him in France. There, he was a broken shell, and she wondered if perhaps his momentary breakdown in the airport stemmed from a fear of leaving. How easy it is to become complacent, Melanie thought, and how terrifying change could be. She had confronted the trials of her own life the way she had because, with Edward gone, she felt the need to be strong and resilient, like he had been. How many times had she come close to breaking? How many times did she feel like giving up, collapsing in tears, but couldn't for Gem's sake? She thought that, with Edward being home, those days were gone. She could feel again, openly, without worrying about showing weakness to Abigail or anyone else.

And yet, even with Edward's return, her guard had to stay up, for his sake now. It was a thought that didn't make her bitter, but made her realize how strong she had always been, how little credit she had given herself, and a resolve to keep that chin up, as the General was prone to say.

But what of this man, this poor wounded man, who

in spite of his condition made his way through a war zone and then found a way to make a living amidst the rubble of Europe. This man who had picked himself up, and marched forward, and after all this time, could sit at a makeshift table and have tea with his little girl. He wasn't lost. He wasn't broken. He was indomitable.

She smiled to herself, feeling an oppressive weight lift from her shoulders. She inhaled a sweet breath of freedom, from their past, from their expectations, from any concerns of what the people in town or her in-laws might think of him now, and appreciated this moment, sitting in her chair, in their house, watching her husband and her daughter enjoy each other under a clear summer sky on a beautiful day.

Father and daughter stayed outside for an hour, coming inside only when Melanie called them for breakfast or lunch or whatever meal time it was. When Edward entered the kitchen, his eyes lit up just as they had when Gem first saw him preparing crepes. Melanie made pancakes which Edward devoured. Gem added cherries for eyes and a nose, and raisins in a sweep for a mouth, her little girl beautiful laugh, so wonderful to hear again. When they finished, Edward looked up at Melanie and smiled, a warm, loving smile that said to Melanie, "I'm happy to be home."

"Mommy, can we go the store?" Gem said.

"Of course, dear. We've been gone for a month." She looked at her husband. "After a nap," she added.

Home.

Edward gave Melanie a look she hadn't seen from him since they had reunited, a look of pleasure—hers, his, theirs. It was a look that every functioning family, with all of its entangled dynamics, its connection and communion, shares in loving silence, in recognition of the limits of language, of words, to express the depth of feeling present among them.

Melanie took Edward by the hand and led him to the bedroom. "This is where you'll be staying," she said looking into his eyes, "with me. I tried to make it look the way we used to have our bedroom in your parent's house, but we have more space here. Maybe one of these days we can buy some more furniture for the room, or your father could make some. He's been wonderful while you've been away. I know that it'll be hard for you, adjusting to this new life, adjusting to us. I just wanted you to know that some things are the same. That my love for you is the same, if not greater. Everything I've accomplished, all the people I've met, all the support we've had over the years, it was empty without you. Even though you've changed, you're still my Edward, and this is our home."

Home.

She grabbed his face and kissed his lips. At first, he didn't respond, and then he slightly pressed back, before softly pulling away. He looked at her lovingly, and tears began to well up in her eyes.

They heard the door to Gem's room close. Melanie took his hand and walked with him over to the bed. She lay down on one side, patted the other side for him to join her. She fell asleep almost instantly, but he stayed awake, observing her face, her hair, her body. He searched his mind for something to click, for all the memories she had told him to come rushing back. It was as though a wall had built up in the back of his brain. All he had were indistinct glimpses, blurred flashes of anything before he had awakened in a desecrated field, surrounded by mutilated corpses.

Home.

Her kiss had felt at once familiar and alien. He wanted her to be his wife, but more than that, he wanted to remember her as his wife. He wanted to touch her, but it didn't feel right. His mind and body ragged from the flight finally took its toll and he slept. A couple of hours later,

Gem came into the room, eager to go to the market.

It was a lovely afternoon. The three of them walked to the market, shopped for groceries, only those that they could carry back easily. Melanie prayed that they wouldn't run into anyone they knew, especially Fred or Abigail. The checker was someone Melanie didn't know and the box boy, about sixteen, had been barely out of childhood when Edward had gone off to war.

The walk home was glorious. Gem skipped and ran and chirped back at the birds, laughing at herself.

Back in the kitchen, Gem set out a mixing bowl, a rolling pin, eggs and milk, butter and flour. Even before Melanie insisted that she put on her apron, the happy little girl had flour in her hair, on her face, and somehow on her shoes. Melanie helped her mix the ingredients, instructing Gem how to cut up the fruit, warning her to be careful with the knife. Edward sat across from them at the table and watched. Melanie said, "We're making hot cross buns with fruit. Gem's recipe."

Gem took her father's hand and showed him how to cut up the fruit, and once the dough was mixed, she showed him how to knead it. Upon touching the dough, he felt something break inside of him, as though a window had opened. Without trepidation, he grabbed the dough and went to work, as though his body was rejoining his spirit with each eager plunge of his fingers through the thickening dough.

Home.

After kneading, they separated the chunks of dough into balls to be rolled out. Melanie was having some difficulty with hers. Edward watched her, pausing, his heart racing. His brain told his hand to move, but it wouldn't respond. Melanie anguished over the dough, her arms straining, frustration reddening her face. For just a moment, he felt himself hanging in time, unsure as to how to break the spell.

As if she knew, as if she could recognize the spell freezing her father and knowing how to break it, Gem stopped her task and slightly brushed across her father's hands resting there on the counter. Edward looked up at her, a smile—the brightest thus far—stretched across his soul. Clumsily lurching out, like a man rediscovering reflexes, he grabbed Melanie's hand. The movement startled her.

Looking quickly up into his eyes, she calmed. She felt his hands on hers. He guided her hand over the rolling pin gently, flattening, turning, flattening, turning. Rolling. His hand stayed on top of hers, and then, ever so slightly, his fingers began to part hers, and her hand went limp as his fingers slid in and clutched her hand into his own. Their hands thus entwined, he pulled their tangle of fingers, a Gordian knot of emotion and love, to his chest and looked her in the eyes. She felt her knees about to buckle just as his arm came around her back, and he leaned in to kiss her.

Home.

He let go of her hand and reached out for Gem, who leapt into his lap to embrace him. Melanie rested her head on his shoulder.

Home.

A fire had been burning deep within him since they boarded the plane in Paris. He hadn't understood it until they arrived at the house. It nearly overwhelmed him when Melanie kissed him, and now, as a wave of memory and emotion swept over him, the trauma of war, the anguish of his injuries, and his fears of being caught, tortured or killed cast aside, he opened his mouth to say: "I love you."

Jean Blasiar is the award-winning author of the Emmy Budd mystery series for young readers, ages 7 to 13, and "Poor Rich" and "Richer" for young adults. Jean's previous experience as a playwright and theatrical producer in the Los Angeles area resulted in one of Jean's plays optioned by Twentieth Century Fox for a pilot.

"Communion" is Jean's first adult novel in collaboration with her editor at Savant, Jonathan Marcantoni. The screenplay for "Communion" has been written by Jean and Jonathan and currently in the hands of an agent and producer.

A freelance writer and editor since 2004, **Jonathan Marcanton**i is a graduate of the University of Tampa, where he majored in Spanish studies. He has worked on The Bleepin Truth television show and also for the Tampa Bay Sun newspaper. He is a Savant editor, residing in San Antonio with his wife and two daughters.

If you enjoyed *Communion* consider these other fine books from
Savant Books and Publications:

A Whale's Tale by Daniel S. Janik
Tropic of California by R. Page Kaufman
The Village Curtain by Tony Tame
Dare to Love in Oz by William Maltese
The Interzone by Tatsuyuki Kobayashi
Today I Am a Man by Larry Rodness
The Bahrain Conspiracy by Bentley Gates
Called Home by Gloria Schumann
Kanaka Blues by Mike Farris
First Breath edited by Zachary M. Oliver
Poor Rich by Jean Blasiar
The Jumper Chronicles by W. C. Peever
William Maltese's Flicker by William Maltese
My Unborn Child by Orest Stocco
Last Song of the Whales by Four Arrows
Perilous Panacea by Ronald Klueh
Falling but Fulfilled by Zachary M. Oliver
Manifest Intent by Mike Farris
The Mythical Voyage by Robin Ymer
Hello, Norma Jean by Sue Dolleris
Richer by Jean Blasiar
Charlie No Face by David Seaburn
Number One Bestseller by Brian Morley
My Two Wives and Three Husbands by S. Stanley Gordon
*In Dire Strait*s by Jim Currie
Wretched Land by Mila Komarnisky
Chan Kim by Ilan Herman
Who's Killing All the Lawyers? by A. G. Hayes
Ammon's Horn by Guerrino Amati
Wavelengths edited by Zachary M. Oliver

Scheduled for Release in 2011:

Blood Money by Scott Mastro
In the Himalayan Nights by Anoop Chandola
Almost Paradise by Laurie Hanan
Random Views of Asia from the Mid-Pacific by William E. Sharp, Jr.

http://www.savantbooksandpublications.com

Made in the USA
Charleston, SC
01 October 2011